I'd never bee[...]
was to shake [...]
other thing to [...]
jump him, gr[...]
wall, slap his [...] way but straight
and beat out of him the name of his boss. Oh,
yeah. There's a third thing you can do. Get
home as fast as your legs can carry you, and
make damned sure you double lock the door.

The phone was ringing as I came in, out of
breath. The voice at the other end was garbled.

'Say it again,' I ordered.

'I said, Art Farquharson was killed last night.'

THE LAST WEDNESDAY

BERNARD BANNERMAN

SPHERE BOOKS LIMITED

A SPHERE BOOK

First published in Great Britain by Sphere Books Ltd 1989

ISBN 0 7474 0382 1

Typeset by Selectmove Ltd., London.
Printed and bound in Great Britain by
Cox & Wyman Ltd, Reading

Sphere Books Ltd
A Division of
Macdonald & Co (Publishers) Ltd
Orbit House
1 New Fetter Lane
London EC4A 1AR
A member of Maxwell Macmillan Pergamon Publishing Corporation

For Pat and Vince
and for Francesca Alicia

Chapter One

'Who's paying you?' she asked.

'How many of you people have got to die before you do something about it?' I didn't answer.

We stared at each other: she gave way first.

I could guess why. She didn't like to look at me. I wasn't a pretty picture. She didn't want to remember.

It was a long time ago that we were together. I had cut a very different figure. I was young, good-looking, bearded, radical, and going places. I weighed about three stone less.

Nowadays, I don't wear a beard, though if I forget to shave for a few days the difference is hard to tell. My politics gave up the ghost when food and drink were in short supply. I don't often have anywhere to go and when I do it takes me ten times as long.

'Are you still practising?'

'Getting near perfect,' I said jauntily but without a great deal of originality.

'Well, anyhow, yes, a bit. I haven't got an office. I do. . . Bits and pieces from home. . .'

I figured: let her go on asking questions. When it got to my turn, she'd owe me some answers.

We were sitting in the Covent Garden Plaza. On the lower deck. Outside the wine bar and rib joint. We used to go there before. It seemed as good a place to meet as any. It wasn't too far from Temple, where her chambers were, and though it wasn't cheap, I was on expenses.

I guess I should have said: Anne's a barrister and the

way I got to know her is that I'm a solicitor. A lot of people don't really understand the difference: solicitors are the ones who rip you off in an office, while barristers sell you out in court. Solicitors work in firms, and barristers work in chambers. There's a bunch more I could tell you, but I doubt you really care, and I know for sure I don't.

'How's chambers going?'

It was a long time since we met. We'd gone in diametrically opposite directions. Like: north and south, up and down. She'd gone up, I'd gone down.

'OK.' She shrugged:

'It doesn't feel like the same place any more, you know...'

Anne was in Alexander Keenan's chambers. Alex Keenan when he wanted to remind you he was just one of the boys. They were – so they claimed – 'special'. One of those chambers which only defended criminals, never prosecuted; they acted for tenants, not landlords; employees not employers; battered women, not the violent man. They were 'political', and proud of it.

Anne could pass for working class. At a pinch. Her father had been a union official. She'd been a social worker first, later took up law. When I knew her, she was about twenty-nine, but still in the last year of her training, as a pupil barrister. Also, heavily feminist, and stridently gay.

She wasn't what you'd call conventionally attractive. As a matter of fact, she wasn't really attractive at all. She was overweight, wore glasses that couldn't have suited her less, and dressed like she was putting out the garbage. But – like everyone else – she didn't like to think of herself as unattractive. Somewhere deep inside of her, the only way she could convince herself she wasn't the next thing to a sack of potatoes was if once in a while she made it with a man.

That was why she'd got it together with me. Among others.

She hadn't changed. In the fifteen minutes and most of a bottle we'd been sitting there, she'd begun to think:

well, maybe he isn't too disgusting, too fat, too bleary-eyed, too embarrassing, to remind herself she could turn men on as well.

I'd changed, though. Some time during the last five years, as I groped feebly to find the safest gutter, I'd lost interest. I don't mean in her particularly (because, after all, I hadn't been that particular about her last time around), but in it all. It wasn't worth the effort.

'Where're you living?' she asked. This was standard. Probe a bit; find out if he or she is living alone; what part of town (after all, and just for example, you'd have to be pretty desperate to go south of the river); is the desire enough to do it in your own home, even if it means waking up with some alien being in your bed, not just having to be polite to them first thing in the morning, but having to fix them coffee, maybe even something to eat.

'Same place,' I answered. I could tell: my answer was no turn on.

I wasn't exactly being honest with Anne. She'd asked if I was practising, and I'd said I was practising from home. She assumed that meant: practising law, as a solicitor.

The last time I did anything as a solicitor was when I sued my former partner for twenty thousand pounds, as my share of our firm, and settled out of court for five hundred.

That was some years ago, soon after Sandy kicked my arse out of the office when I turned up strung out on cocaine at two o'clock in the afternoon while she'd spent the morning explaining to some handjob in a funny red gown and a horse-hair wig to cover his remaining few hairs why it was we hadn't prepared the case, told the client (for which read: thieving little bastard) he was due in court to watch the scales of justice come down against him, or instructed a barrister to put up a show our villain could complain about while he spent the next five years sewing mailbags.

Yeah, I was still in the same place. In all manner of ways. Same home. Same clothes (you'd be surprised

3

how they last when you ain't got any money). Same waiting around for my father to die and leave me enough money to take off for some place else. Same disillusionment with law, the legal system, lawyers and – above all – so-called left-wing lawyers, getting a healthy living off pretending to fight the state on behalf of the oppressed and all along taking away from the victim the one true solace he or she ever had: they never gave me a chance.

So I'd given up law, more or less. Instead, I hung my shingle out as what the glossies call a private eye. I put my name in the yellow pages. (Let your fingers do the walking. Let your money do the talking.) I advertised in the legal press: 'confidential enquiries and process serving by qualified solicitor.'

Now I'll give you the time of day for free if you can tell me which I got more of: the confidential enquiries, or the process serving? You got it. In the last three years, I hung about outside more council houses than you've had bad hamburgers, waiting for some violent husband to show up, so's I could overawe, overwhelm and overpower him with the majesty of the law by hitting him on the nearest part of his anatomy with a bit of funny parchment that's got Latin written all over it and that tells him he ain't allowed to beat up on his wife any more, and run like hell.

I'd like to say: I've scraped by. I'd like to say that to give you the idea I ain't the lazy, incompetent slob I'm making myself out to be, but a modest, unassuming bloke, rich in integrity, downplaying his achievements. Unfortunately, neither would be true. I haven't scraped by (anyhow, on what I've earned), and I sure as hell ain't modest, unassuming or rich in integrity.

I'd place the time at about three or four months before this meet with Anne I've left you in the middle of that I can set my hand on my heart, wait for it to calm down, and assure you that I'd definitely stopped scraping by. Meaning? Meaning I owed more money than I could dream of. Meaning that if the people I owed it to were clean, decent, down-to-earth capitalists who understood what a fine and proper and natural thing it was to go bankrupt, that's where I would've been. Meaning, the people I owed money to weren't clean, decent or down-to-earth. Where they lived was about fifty feet below.

One of the reasons I'm so scathing about south of the river (the other is some residual sense of good taste) is because I live so close to it. I live on Redcliffe Square, which some of the residents like to call – imaginatively – West Chelsea, an area of London no cab-driver ever heard of. The rest of London knows it as Earl's Court, otherwise Kangaroo Valley from years ago when all the Aussies used to hang out there, otherwise Fag Alley.

You don't need a lot of insider information to work out why it's called Fag Alley. That's where all the gays live. Well, maybe not all of them, but enough to seem like it. And certainly all the gays of a particular type: leather-jacketed, slightly balding, moustachioed, the sort you wake up in the middle of the night and find pissing on your carpet – or you.

But what people don't know quite so well is that it's got its own mob. By mob I mean exactly what you think I mean. Gangsters. Hoodlums. Thugs. The only difference between them and the best the East End has to offer is that they slit your arse open before they cut your balls off. They're into all the usual rackets. Gambling. Prostitution (female, male, and who knows or cares). Drugs (soft or hard). They lend money, too.

Of course, only a fool borrows from them. Only a fool, or a down-and-out solicitor with vague expectations of a timely parental death and whose brain ain't working too good. (You are wondering: what's the difference? 'Are the two mutually exclusive?' I hear you cry. There is a difference, though. The solicitor is qualified, a professional person, he is educated. That means: he does things the same way a fool does. But. He gets the chance to do a whole lot more of them).

About ten months ago I borrowed five hundred quid from one of these Earl's Court community workers. Even I knew it was a pretty stupid thing to do, but, I guess, if you're born lucky you'll find your way out of any mess, and if you're born unlucky it won't make that much difference.

About five months ago, this community worker's colleagues came around to my Redcliffe Square basement in order to discuss my problems with me. Specifically: why I hadn't paid back the money.

I told them about my mother dying ten years ago. That didn't impress them. I told them my youngest sister was a drug addict. That didn't impress them either. I told them my oldest sister was a schoolteacher. One of them was a wee bit shocked, but it still didn't make a real difference. I told them my father was bound to die some day: they asked if I'd put a contract out on him. Finally, we reached an agreement: I told them I'd pay them back within the week.

Now this is where else fools and solicitors are different. A fool couldn't've done what I did. I don't say he wouldn't have thought of it. He just wouldn't have had the chance. I went to see my bank manager. He was pleased to see me. He was another community worker, concerned about my problems. I told him a different story than I'd told the other lot. I told him I was past all my difficulties. I told him I was going back to work. I told him I'd had an offer from a property company, that I could handle their portfolio if I set up in practice again. I told him that was what I was going to do.

People don't understand banks. They're frightened of asking for money from the bank manager. Like, a loan. They think every time they're overdrawn the bank manager breathes fire and puts his commandoes on red alert. Wrong. Consider. Just for a moment. You're a nice, sweet, respectable, responsible person. You earns your money and you pays your keep. Maybe once ten years ago you wrote out a cheque that might've bounced if the multi-national corporation or local authority you work for happened to go bust before they paid your wages. That's about the worst you ever did. How much do you pay the bank?

Right. You don't pay the bank peanuts. If you got

6

more than the next month's mortgage payment sitting in your account, you don't get charged for nothing. No charge per transaction. No charge for cheques drawn or paid in. No charge for standing orders. No charge for having an account. They even send you those pretty little books and plastic cards with magnetic strips on them free of charge. (If you ask nicely, they give you neat little covers for them – also, free of charge.) You ain't worth sweet fanny adams to the bank.

Where do you think banks get their money from? They get it from lending it. They get it from overdrafts they've terrified people into thinking they have to pay back. They get it from taking risks. Not too great a risk, mind you, 'cos the bank manager who doesn't get the right rate of returns ain't gonna be lending in South Kensington for much longer. (I'm told that in Hackney you can borrow a fiver if you leave your car as security.) That's what bank managing is about. Calculating risks. If you're a good risk, there's no limit to what you can have. If you're a bad risk, well, you might still pay some of it back.

That's what I did. I borrowed money from my bank manager to re-establish myself as a solicitor. He lent it me to re-establish myself as a solicitor. Also, he lent it me because my family has been banking with his lot since before his father'd started dreaming about someone to carry on the clerking. But he lent it me.

My community worker was impressed. It's interesting. Money gets you money. Also, it gets you respect. He said to me: 'How come you didn't pay up before?' I said: 'It was tied up.' Suddenly. I didn't do a volte face in his eyes; it was more like a pirouette. I was no longer a bum he was extorting 20% per month from, but an institution he was investing in. He said: 'You and I should get together. We should get to know each other better. We should get real close.' I looked down at his pants. A thing like that could hurt. I passed up the opportunity.

There is, of course, an inconsistency in what I have chosen to reveal to you thus far. On the one hand, I have admitted lying to Anne Godwin about 'practising'. On the other, I'm telling you how I financially organized myself back into practice as a solicitor. There is a solution, if you read the small print. I didn't say that in fact I'd gone back into practice as a solicitor.

The solution, such as it is, poses a problem you'll have worked out for yourself. I had to come up with money, to pay the bank with (or go bankrupt. I should have mentioned: a bankrupt solicitor gets what is quaintly called 'struck off the roll'. For those of you who don't know what that spells, I get to not be a solicitor any more. In turn, I get to not borrow from the bank any more. Around and around.)

Now, funnily enough, by some sort of coincidence, how I burrowed my way out of that one and how I came to be back in Covent Garden drinking wine with Fat Annie, and wondering if my client would believe a meal on expenses, have just a little bit in common. I'll tell you about it.

It didn't happen suddenly. For about two months, I lived pretty high off the bank. My bank manager wasn't that much of a fool. I mean. He'd done one pretty dumb thing. Lending me money. But he wasn't so stupid as to think it'd start pouring back in the very next day. (As a matter of fact, it would've been a disaster if it had. The whole point was – remember – to make a profit out of it, i.e. interest. Just in case, or 'cos he got the wobblies, he sent me a couple of clients. I had to lie my way out of acting for them without explaining I didn't have a current practice certificate any more, and hadn't paid the compulsory professional insurance.)

Then for another couple of months I worked really hard at process-serving. I touted for work like crazy. I rang every solicitor I'd ever acted for and hustled them for work. I slapped parchment on more bums than I care to remember. I got hit by three of them, but only one of them hurt more than my pride. One of the advantages of being fat is people aren't too sure if you're strong, or just overweight.

Process-serving was, of course, getting me nowhere.

I was about ready to think in terms of an extended vacation abroad, and I wouldn't have been sending my bank manager a postcard. Maybe I'd sting the community worker for a bit of 'investment money'. Split was on my mind.

Then I got a call. Funny thing. Just before that call, I would've said I'd used up all my chances (and there weren't that many to begin with). Right after, I had this feeling I was on my feet bigger than when I'd been at the height of my (so-called) career. Funnier still: I was right.

'Can I speak with' (note, not 'to') 'Mr Woolf please. . .'

'Who's calling?' (I did my imitation of Lily Tomlin. It wasn't hard. I was picking my nose at the time.)

'I don't think he'll know my name, It's Mrs Nicholas. Is Mr Woolf available?'

'I'll see for you, Mrs Nicholas.' (Leaving my finger stuck up my snozzle meant extra pickings.) 'Can you tell me what it's in connection with?'

'Oh. I see. Perhaps. . . Perhaps you would remind him he once stayed in my house. In Wiltshire.'

I thought fast. She sounded too old for someone I'd slept with. I was certain (well, as near as I could be), it wasn't someone I'd borrowed money from. Wiltshire? I hadn't ever been in Wiltshire. For a start. It's south of the river. Isn't it? I was getting about ready to tell her I wasn't available when she said:

'Is that Mr Woolf?'

Wily old bitch.

'I'll put you through now,' I sneered.

'Mrs Nicholas? David Woolf here. How can I help you?' My voice dropped three octaves.

'You don't remember me, do you Mr Woolf.' It wasn't a question.

'Well, I'm. . . Er. . . Or course. . . That is to say. . .' I wasn't normally lost for words.

'There's no reason why you should,' she added quickly:

'You stayed in my house, a few years ago, with my son Jack. . .'

9

Now that was a name that rang a bell: Jack Nicholas. I was sure I knew it. I just wasn't sure why. It wasn't 'cos it sounded like Jack Nicholson. It wasn't 'cos it sounded like Jack Nicklaus. Just in time, I remembered: he was someone I'd been at school with.

'No, I don't think you were at school with my son. . .'

Wrong again.

'My son was a barrister. His chambers came to our home. A sort of, well, he called it a chambers' outing. I think. . . Your wife. . . One of the members?'

My wife? I hadn't been married. Ever. Had I?

It was enough, though, to put me on the right lines: Anne Godwin; chambers; Jack Nicholas – they used to call him the Jackdaw, the way his head was shaped, and he'd talk – lecture or argue, I never heard him do anything else – his head bobbing at you like he was stealing the eyes out of your skull.

'Yes, of course,' I lied: 'I'm sorry I didn't recall. How are you Mrs Nicholas?' I cared about as much as I cared if it was raining outside.

'Thank you. Yes. I was wondering. . . I gather you're not practising, as a solicitor. . . Any more. . . But. . . I saw an advertisement. . . In a magazine. . . Would it be, the Law Society's Journal?'

'Law Society's Gazette. Solicitor's Journal. Yes, I advertise in both of them. Could have been either.' She wanted me for one of two things: confidential enquiries, or process-serving. The odds were stacked in favour of the latter.

'Yes. Thank you.' What a grateful lady, I thought.

'You read about my son? You weren't at the funeral, I think. Of course,' she added quickly: 'There was no reason why you should have been. You weren't that close. But your wife was there. . .'

There are times when even I am impressed by my intellect. I worked out the Jackdaw was dead.

'I, er, well, she wasn't my wife. . .' Was all I said. It wouldn't've caused me convulsions to say I was sorry the jerk was dead. I just never thought of it.

'Oh. Yes. Thank you.'

Stop with the thank-yous, I screamed silently.

'I was wondering. . . Would it be possible. . . To see you, Mr Woolf? On a. . . Well, confidential matter. . .'

Like: confidential as in confidential enquiries? Hell, yes, no one wanted to see me on one of them before. I didn't even know what they looked like.

We arranged to meet in exactly a week's time. She would, she said, be in town in any event, and she would rather see me while she was already up. She didn't say: it would be more convenient to see you while I'm in town anyway. More like: when I have another excuse to be in town.

We were going to meet in Harrods tea-room. That was good for me for two reasons. First of all, it was near enough for me to walk, which saved the bus-fare. Secondly, I could tell her it was near where I 'was' (she wasn't to know if she was talking to my office or my home). If I was near Harrods, I might well be (for all she knew) in an office in South Kensington, or Knightsbridge, or – even! – Belgravia.

'How will I know you?' I remembered to ask.

'I'll remember you, Mr Woolf. I never forget a face.'

I thought: this may be it. Five years ago, there was only one face to remember. Now, there were at least two faces, and a handful of chins.

Part of me expected her to no-show. It could be a gag, from the one or two people I'd stayed in touch with who had followed my decline with cathartic attention to detail. Or, she might have chickened out. Most likely of all, no one went to Harrods for tea any more, the store worked their way through the telephone directory to book dates with suckers like me who'd've ordered something they had to pay for before they worked out it was a con.

'Mr Woolf?' A lady of about fifty-five, greying hair, and wearing an extremely large hat, hovered over me. Her hair was what they called blue-rinsed. She was wearing a dark grey suit. She looked so smart she could've been one of my mother's friends.

'Right. Mrs Nicholas?' I remembered something I'd

11

been taught at school between Latin and cricket and bending over for the house bully: I stood up.

'I did have difficulty remembering you,' she admitted: 'You've changed.'

Meaning. I was fat. My suit was worn and had forgotten the name of my neighbourhood cleaner. My shoes would've fainted at the sight of boot-black. But. I had shaved. With a blunt razor, admittedly, but no one could say I had more than a six o'clock shadow.

It was three o'clock.

'Can I get you some tea?' I offered. I hadn't used all the bank's money yet, though tea at Harrods might well take care of what was left.

'I think that must be for me to do, thank you,' she said quietly.

She meant. First, she had sussed out I didn't have any money. Secondly, we weren't meeting socially – I wasn't, eh, wot, a gentleman taking a lady to tea – but professionally, and she was the client, for which read she was about to buy me.

I inclined my head with what I hope looked like graciousness but was thinking how many days can I survive on cream cakes.

After the wally in the waistcoat had dumped the silver salver, and Mrs Nicholas had played mother (she'd just lost a child, it was the least I could let her do), we got down to business with a directness that would've made my community worker look like he was dissembling.

'Did you know my son Jack had died? Before I telephoned, I mean?'

'Well, no, to tell the truth.' (Buy me tea at Harrods and I'll tell you no lies.)

'I, uh, don't move in the same circles any more. . .'

'I gathered.' She was no dufus. (Dufus = jerk = dumbo = idiot = someone who lives south of the river = etc.)

'He died five weeks ago.'

She paused. For a second there, I thought she was waiting for me to say something. Then I realized it was deliberate. She was weighing things up in her mind.

12

Like. Once she said what came next, a secret idea had turned real.

'I want you to investigate his death, Mr Woolf. I want you to find out. . .how it happened. . .' Then. In a whisper. She added:

'I want you to find out who did it, Mr Woolf. . .'

I swallowed hard. The back of my throat was dry. My hand was trembling too much to hold a cup. This sort of thing didn't happen. Any more. At least. Not to me.

'You. Want. Me. To. Find. Out. How. Your. Son. Died? OK?'

'Yes. That's correct, Mr Woolf. I'll pay, of course,' she added quickly, as if my hesitation might be on account of I thought she was asking me to do it as a favour. Like. For staying in her house maybe?

To myself I repeated the words over. She wants me to find out how her son died.

I was caught between two conflicting impulses. I oughta put as much distance between myself and this fruitcake as I could. And. There could be a lotta loot in it.

I needed time to think:

'Uh, maybe you should tell me what happened?'

She nodded slowly. Picked up her cup. By the handle. Between thumb and forefinger. Little pinky stuck right out at me. It looked sort of lonely.

She sipped her tea. Quietly. Not a slurp, not a gulp. The way if other people ate or drank I might just have found them a bit more tolerable to have around. Then she told me.

'He died in an accident. He was on his bicycle. It was on a Wednesday, the twenty-fifth of last month. It happened at a quarter to eleven. He was on his way home from his chambers.'

The big deal wasn't exactly crystal clear.

'He had carried his bicycle on to the train and only had a short distance to go to reach home.'

At least she was giving me plenty of time to think. It was about as interesting as an advert for Kelloggs' cornflakes.

13

'I think I ought to say, the police said he was intoxicated.'

For the first time, she was talking a language I understood.

'The driver did not stop. He hasn't been found.'

The spaces between sentences made it seem like it was a subject she found hard to talk about. For some reason.

'There was an inquest. His head of chambers represented us. Alexander Keenan. You know him of course,' she added flatly.

I guess. It depends what you mean by know. I wouldn't exactly say: kissing cousins.

Another pause. Longer than the ones before. I sussed she was getting to the real point. Like I said: impressive intellect.

'My son. . . Jack. . . He was. . . He was a very careful man, Mr Woolf. Even as a child. He was well-behaved, never in trouble, always cautious. It may. . . It may even be that he carried it to a fault.'

To a fault? Heaven forfend.

'What was the verdict?' I wanted to get her back on the track. I needed a eulogy to Jackdaw like a hole in the head.

'Thank you. Accidental death. But. . . But it was really that he had died. . . As a result of drink. . . I do not dispute that he had been drinking. I am in no position to do so. There was a blood sample. Some of his colleagues had been drinking with him. But it seemed to be all that the coroner paid any attention to. He kept saying how dangerous it could be on a bicycle, because people only think about the dangers of driving a car in drink.'

I nodded sombrely, suppressing a smile at the quaint old expression 'in drink'.

'I. . . I felt he was using my son's death, Mr Woolf. Using it to make his point.'

I shrugged: 'Coroners like to see their names in the newspapers. . .'

'Yes. Thank you. I understand that. But he wasn't

really interested. . . in how Jack died. I felt. . . I felt none of them were, Mr Woolf. None of them,' she repeated, and for once I was ahead of her: none of them, including Jackdaw's colleagues.

'You see. . . What I said about being careful: he had been drinking, so he took the train home most of the way. That was Jack. If he had been too drunk to travel on his bike, he would have walked from the station.'

'Maybe.'

It wasn't enough to mount a state trial on. The police said he was too drunk to be riding his bike. There were independent witnesses who said he'd been drinking. To me it added up like the guy was simply too drunk to be out on a bike, and here was a mother who didn't want to have to carve on a gravestone: 'To a loving son Jackdaw. Dead, drunk and incapable.'

She read my thoughts. Like an open book. I was really bad at this private eye game.

'Is. . . Is there a Mr Nicholas?' I was playing for more time to think. I remembered the 'phone call: she'd wanted an excuse to be in town, other than me.

'Yes. My husband, Jack's father, is the Reverend Nicholas of St Thomas'. He does not know I am seeing you,' she answered my barely concealed question. She went on to answer the next one without being asked, too:

'My husband is a highly-regarded figure in the church, Mr Woolf. You are not a church-goer, I think?'

'No, I'm Jewish.'

'Ah, yes, thank you. We are a very tolerant family, Mr Woolf. I think – I hope – that's where Jack got his own tolerance from. . .'

It's always the first thing they tell you: they don't mind.

'He has. . . He has a philosophical bent. . .' She was back on the Very Rev:

'It has been a considerable strength in our lives. He believes – a lot of people find it difficult to accept that

15

this is a sufficient explanation for the vicissitudes of life – that what happens is truly God's will. . .'

I wanted to ask: what does vy-sissy-tunes mean? Fag music?

'No more than I does my husband believe that Jack was drunk when he. . . When he had his accident. . . But. . . But he believes it was God's will, and it does not disconcert him not to know more about what happened. . .'

'But it disconcerts you, right?' I thought I might as well show I'd been listening. As well as eating.

She nodded slowly:

'Yes. It does disconcert me.'

Vengeance is mine, saith the mother.

For the second time, she read my thoughts:

'I don't know, Mr Woolf. I don't know why I'm doing this. I don't know why I'm seeing you. I may. . . I am not stupid, Mr Woolf. I know I am a mother who has lost her son. I know I am in grief. But something. . . Just a feeling. . . A mother's intuition if you will. . . I have to know exactly what happened. . . He had. . . He had so much to live for. He was brilliant. I know one should not lightly use the word. He was married: he had a charming wife, a beautiful son. . .'

'Mrs Nicholas. . . Forgive me. . . A lot of people with a whole lot to live for got drunk and died in a crash. . . Others too. . .' Those without so much to live for.

I don't know what made me speak my mind like that. I certainly wasn't acting like I needed her money. Maybe I was getting a little frightened. If I took her money, if I took the case, I'd have to start working on it. I didn't like the idea of poking around someone's grave. You never knew where the body'd been.

She wasn't even remotely thrown by what I'd said. She even smiled a little, for the first time since she'd arrived:

'Yes. Thank you. I'm glad you said that. I told you that I have had those thoughts for myself. If you hadn't said that, I should have had somewhat less confidence in you. . . I should have thought you were

16

just. . . Is 'taking the case' the right expression? For the money. . .'

'Don't let yourself be bought for a one-liner, lady,' I said. I'd meant to say it to myself but I said it out loud.

There was a long silence. My riposte had hardened her resolve. I was her man and she was certain of it.

To fill the gap between the waistcoat asking if we wanted another pot, and bringing it, I said to her:

'Why'd'you choose me?'

'I saw your advertisement. In a magazine in my son's house. It seemed. . .like a sign,' she added quietly.

'How'd you recognize my name? It's been a long time.'

'I thought I recognized it. When I got home I looked it up.'

'You looked it up?'

'In the visitors' book,' she added, as if it was obvious.

'Ah, right.' And I truly did remember. Theirs was the only house I was ever in which had a visitor's book.

After she'd poured more tea I asked:

'If your husband doesn't know. . . How're you going to pay me?'

'I have private money, Mr Woolf. It's not my husband's. He knows about it, of course, but he has always insisted I keep it to myself. I would. . . I would have left it to Jack. . . Now I shall leave it to Phillip. . .' She caught my question again:

'His son. . . But. . . It doesn't matter. I don't need to explain, do I? You need to know I can afford your services. That's all, isn't it?'

'Well, I guess I need to know you didn't rob a bank. . .'

For the very first time, she laughed:

'I didn't rob a bank, Mr Woolf. What are your charges?'

I didn't answer for a moment. She probably thought I was deciding what was fair. Truth was, it was the first time I'd ever had the choice. Process-serving was all fixed-rate. I tried to think. The tea got in my way.

'It's one hundred a day. . .plus expenses.' I only just remembered to add the bit about expenses.

She didn't bat an eyelid. I should've said a hundred fifty.

There was one thing left unclear, which I never got around to asking her. If I had, I doubt she could've answered. Was she saying she wanted to know how he died, and who was involved? Or. Was she saying someone killed him? Killed as in murdered.

Chapter Two

Remember how that programme used to begin? 'There are ten million people in the naked city. . .' (I think it was ten.) Well, there's eight million in London.

Looking for someone who'd knocked someone else off a bicycle was like looking for the proverbial needle in a haystack.

There are only two ways to do it. One is to keep the pressure on, and hope the needle pops out like a squirt of pus from a pimple. The other is to set fire to the haystack and sift the cinders. If the needle still no-shows, there's only two explanations. It wasn't there to begin with. Or. You ain't that good at looking.

I got a bunch more information from the holy man's lady wife before we split. Basic stuff. Like where Jack had lived. What he'd been working at. History. His course in life from public school to the bar. Did he leave any money?

I found out his money went to his wife in trust for the kid. I remembered his wife. She was a lawyer too, a solicitor and very rich in her own right. As for the kid, even the son of two lawyers was unlikely to have killed his father before he reached the age of four.

Everything she told me spelled out just how good the Jackdaw had been. He was close to his family, didn't cheat on his wife, and he had devoted his life to those less fortunate than himself. His father wasn't the only one on talking terms with God: Jack and his wife were active Christians.

Of course, he'd had the breaks. He had come from a

wealthy family, strictly top drawer. He had gone to one of the best public schools, where he had been a prefect and then either head of his house or head of the school, I never did catch which. He'd gone to Oxford. After Oxford, the Council of Legal Education to read for his bar finals. Then pupilage in a commercial set a relative arranged for him. He had every reason to be confident that he would move on and up at the bar at his usual pace.

What I learned from his mother told me his confidence had not been misplaced. He had appeared as a barrister in the House of Lords, in the Court of Appeal, some of his cases had been reported in The Times. The chambers had continued to grow. He had been, until his death, a senior member of the group, one of Keenan's closest confidantes. The younger members, in pupilage or just out, came to him for advice and guidance. He loved to help them. I can bet he left them in no doubt just how much he loved to help them.

He'd even been big enough for his death to get a mention in some of the legal press. 'The name will be familiar to many of our readers. He had the rare skill of making what is for many an obscure subject interesting. . .' The writer didn't have the same skill and I didn't finish the piece.

It wasn't a whole lot to go on. I tried another tack. Retraced his steps the night he died, from Blackfriars to Dalston Junction on the train, then along the Balls Pond Road, which became St Paul's Road, to where he and his family lived in a four storey house overlooking Highbury Fields. I stood outside the house and thought for a long time: finally I figured – maybe three hundred grand.

I didn't go in. I might have been able to get away with 'just passing – offer condolences' to Penny Nicholas, but I wanted to keep the shot for later. I still wasn't clear enough in my own head where I was going, and what I was after.

I was, as they say, getting nowhere fast. I didn't really have a clue what I was doing. I was trained a lawyer.

That meant applying the lawbooks to my client's case. There were no textbooks for this one. I wasted the best part of a week after my visit to the Nicholas' house in Highbury pondering and analysing – like I had a case to present in court – what was the best way to go about it.

I set out on a sheet of paper all I knew about Jackdaw. It didn't cover a single side. I set out on another sheet of paper all the people we knew in common, and who I was still in touch with. That didn't cover a single side either. I set out on another sheet of paper all the different approaches I might adopt. I gave up wasting paper.

Another line was as fruitless as the visit to his house. I rang the cops:

'I'm afraid you'll have to make a formal request for information, sir.'

There was no: my local's the Red Lion, my poison's a large scotch and my mouth can be opened for a fiver slipped across the table under a newspaper open at the racing form. A formal request meant a letter to the Commissioner. I wondered what the Commissioner drank.

There was, however, one mouth that opened easily the moment I gave it an ear. That was the coroner. People in England don't understand the coroner system. They think coroners operate like judges. Detached, distant, inaccessible, addressed only by lawyers, thoroughly biased. I'd found out years ago they function in a different way: investigative, they'll talk and listen to anyone who's got anything to say about a case they're handling, and then they'll decide it the way they'd already made up their minds in the first place.

I knew the coroner for the area where Jack Nicholas died. I had met him years before on a case. A house of bedsitting rooms burned down. I represented the kin of a Kentucky Fried Special: three limbs, deep fried. They seemed to think the landlord was to blame. Something to do with too many people, lousy wiring, cardboard walls, no fire escapes and the last time the extinguishers were inspected was when the owner'd bought the job lot second-hand. It had been a big enough case (meaning: the coroner'd got enough headlines) for him to remember me, and to agree to see me.

'Come along in Woolf. . . How can I help you?'

I'd forgotten what a pretentious prick he was. 'Woolf.' That sort of handle had gone out a hundred years ago. He was – as many coroners are – both a doctor and a barrister. This one was young, black-haired, wearing a dress jacket and grey-striped trousers, a gold watch-chain across his slender belly. He placed his glasses carefully on the leather blotter. Locked his fingers as if in prayer. Waited.

'You handled the inquest on a friend of mine. Jack Nicholas. A barrister. Got killed on his bicycle. Do you remember?'

'Yes, of course. It was only a few weeks ago. I didn't know he was a friend of yours. . .'

The sentence trailed off as he realized how ridiculous it sounded: why or how the hell could he have known. Even if it had been true.

'You, uh, found the accident had happened because he'd been drinking?'

'Good lord no. The verdict was accidental death. If I'd been certain it was caused by drunkenness, I might even have directed a verdict of death by misadventure.' He looked perplexed, as if he genuinely did not recall that drink had figured in the case.

'I was told. . . You had a lot to say about. . .'

'My dear Woolf. That's entirely different. Of course I did. The fellow had been drinking, you know. Quite a lot as I recall. But. . . No, drinking had nothing to do with the verdict. One must. . . After all. . . How shall I put it? Well,' he smiled and held out his hands, not so much in supplication as if welcoming me to the club:

'Use one's opportunities. Bit less of a wasted life, eh, if one can say something to save others. . .'

She had said Jack's father was a vicar, hadn't she? Not a coroner.

'Had he. . . Well, how drunk was he?'

The coroner shrugged:

'Enough. I don't remember. I say, Woolf, you are just here because he was a friend, aren't you?'

Gentlemen and lawyers have one thing in common. They don't lie to one another. Not so's anyone can find out.

'Of course, of course. I know the family. It caused. . . Some distress, shall we say?'

'The remarks about alcohol. I see. I did. . . I did think of that, of course. I could tell that the mother was upset, but that was only natural. The father. . . A churchman, I believe?'

He was checking to see if I really did know the family.

'Yeah. St Thomas'.'

'He seemed. . . Very stoical. . . You don't encounter that as much these days,' he added wistfully.

After a second, he went on: 'But the principal reason I believed it was fair to say what I did was Alexander Keenan. You know him of course.'

Everyone so took it for granted I knew him he was beginning to feel like an old friend, instead of someone I'd only met a few times, a number of years ago.

'What about him?' He'd had his one bite at checking me out.

He frowned. The lines on his brow furrowed. It created a splendid impression. Profound thought. Weighty consideration.

'You know what a trial is like, even in my little court. . .'

For 'little court' read the place he ruled like it was the turnstile at the Pearly Gate.

'There's a certain amount of. . . exchange between bench and bar. . .' He was likening himself to a judge, sitting 'on the bench'. I got his point.

'One indicates what one is thinking. . . The direction one might take. . . It's all, how shall I put it, understood. The public don't follow, of course, but one says one thing, and counsel knows how to react, to tell you whether or not he's going to go on and fight the point, or whether he can live with it. . .'

It wasn't a foreign language. Quite. It was long enough ago I'd done it last time I had to remind myself how it worked. The judge might say:

'One could interpret the position in this way, Mr Woolf . . . Your client. . .' Did/did not mean to do this or that = is/is not guilty of the offence.

In reply you say:

'With respect, sir, I would have thought. . .' Meaning you won't buy it. Or:

'Quite, sir. That's something that's clearly open to you. In law, that would mean that my client would be not guilty as charged, although guilty, perhaps, of the lesser offence of. . .'

It's all very proper. Nor is it confined to a final finding. It's: 'why don't we tackle this bit of it like this or that. . .' A highly skilled judge knows exactly when to start extracting agreements from counsel, a little bit at a time, until, like a chess game, he can get the result he wants:

'Given what you accepted an hour ago must have happened on the 5th, Mr Woolf, and given the provisions of section thirty-eight, wouldn't you think I'd be bound to find against you?'

Uh. Er. Um.

(People think lawyers fight each other. Bullshit. One or other of them is fighting the judge. Who has already decided which side he's on.)

What the coroner was telling me was that he'd early on decided to dress the Jackdaw's death up as death by drunken biking, and Keenan had acquiesced. The question was:

'Why did you want to take it that way?'

'It seemed to me. . . That was what it was about. There was an oddity. After all, the fellow had put his bike on the train. The journey must have sobered him up. The rest of the route was well-known to him. It isn't that busy a road at that time of the night. It wasn't that far to go.'

Right. That was what his mother thought. But. My question stood.

'He was. . . Have you seen the photographs?'

I shook my head. I remember seeing a seven-by-eight glossy of my client in the bedsit case. It didn't turn me on.

'He was very badly damaged. . .'

Maybe after all he wasn't dead. Just returned to manufacturer for repair.

'The collision was clearly head-on. Very hard. Very fast, I would have said.'

'Is that what the police said?'

'Er, not in court. . .'

He meant: yes, in his own room, where I was talking to him. It was all, of course, off the record, what the papers call 'unattributable'.

'So why? You haven't answered my question. . .'

'No more I have,' he said softly, reminding me he wasn't obliged to see me, let alone to tell me any of this. It could also have been read as: I haven't told you anything.

He brought the tips of his fingers together in a spire. He was thinking. He was wondering whether to go on talking to me. Eventually, he must have decided. He'd gone this far. If he clammed up now, it'd look as if he had something to hide.

'The alternative. . . Unlawful killing. Death by person or persons unknown? Would that have helped the family? Would it have helped anyone? What would we have been talking about? Manslaughter,' meaning death by reckless driving:

'Not murder, to be sure. . .'

'To be sure?'

For the very first time he began to think he maybe ought to be listening to me, instead of the other way round:

'Do you know something, Woolf? Are you holding something back?'

25

'Is it impossible?'

'Have you got any evidence? Anything? Even a motive?'

I shook my head:

'No. I just want to know.'

His eyebrows furrowed. Irreverently I thought: those are fine eyebrows; they belong on an actor. Or a politician.

He was thinking: I was behaving like more than a friend, curious about an accidental death. But he was locked in to the conversation and too stupid to find a way out of it.

'There was no reason. . . I accept it was an odd accident. But odd accidents do happen. There was nothing else to go on. The police wanted to shut the file. Keenan was content. For me to have held out would have been. . . Arrogant?'

I would've thought that was the one reason he would've insisted on a different line.

I was going to get nothing more out of him. For all his pomp and circumstance, he was just one more cog in the machine, helping the wheels turn smoothly. If I hadn't long ago sussed out all lawyers were creeps, I might just've felt a bit sick.

He did two things for me, though. First, he had confirmed the information I'd been given by Mrs Reverend: there were peculiarities about the accepted version of Jack's death; and, Keenan himself had been happy to go along with it.

I knew now where I was heading. The chambers. I rang as soon as I got home:

'Can I speak to Anne Godwin, please?'

'She's not here.'

I always love the friendly, helpful attitude adopted by left-wingers. It's part of the spirit of collectivism. It's not my job to be nice. It's his. Or hers.

'Can I leave a message?'

Silence.

'Can you tell her Dave Woolf rang?'

Something clicked with whoever was at the other end.

26

Dave Woolf. A distant name. But. A solicitor. Solicitors bring barristers work. That made me important.

'I'm terribly sorry, she's on holiday. Can I help you at all? Did you want to instruct her?' Meaning: brief her, meaning bring her some work, and them some loot.

'No. I'm an old friend. When will she be back?'

'Hold on a minute. There's another call.' I might as well have said I was the tax inspector.

But. I was tying up a line. A mere ten or fifteen minutes later, the mongoloid got back to me.

'Who was it you wanted to speak to?' She asked.

'Lev Bronstein, if he's around.'

'Who?'

'Anne Godwin. You said she was on holiday. When will she be back?'

'Oh. She's only just gone. . .' I heard her call out to one of her fellow clerks: 'How long's Anne gone away for, Jo?'

I spent another five telephone units establishing it would be at least two more weeks before Anne would get back.

If I'd still been in practice as a solicitor, trying to brief her, it would have been a good excuse to do nothing about the case for a while. If I was genuinely only calling up as a friend, it wouldn't've mattered. But I had a lot of money to make in a hurry. I needed to keep the clock running.

After I hung up, I wondered what one of the great American detectives would've done in my situation. I didn't have a gun. Or a fast car. Or a leggy blonde girlfriend.

Me? I opened a bottle of wine. Then I put a tape in the cassette player. Listened to Beethoven. The fifth. I'd drunk half a bottle by the time he reached the glorious second movement. It was my favourite sound in the whole wide world, heard that way.

Next stop was even better. I skimmed the evening paper and found a treat. I'd been so hyped up on seeing the coroner I'd forgotten what day it was. Hill Street Blues. Even better. There was no technician's strike. The programme wasn't just listed in the paper. It would actually be broadcast.

I took my phone off the hook and settled in for an hour's visit to my spiritual home. Maybe I'd get some help from Captain Furillo, Howard Hunter ('Now we've got a problem here. Jack Nicholas is of the dead persuasion,') or Mick Belcher, with whom I identified most of all, except for some extraordinary reason he seemed actually to like his parents.

I wasn't far out either. Mick gave me my clue. He was setting up some hoods who were trying to milk the owner of a fish-market. Put his mike in the mouth of a salmon trout. The point was, as he always did, he went undercover, took up the role of a fish-salesman himself. By the time I switched off – wishing I was rich enough to buy a video so's I could watch it all over again and any evening I liked – I knew which way I was going.

It was strange walking back in through the swing doors of Keenan's chambers. He had the whole top floor of a building in the Middle Temple. Middle Temple? It's one of the four Inns of Court where almost all the barristers practising in London work.

Inns of Court? Well, hell, I don't know how to describe them. This ain't an introduction to the English legal system: I just know all barristers have to belong to an Inn. They're like freemasons and elks and other clubs who wouldn't have me as a member even if I could afford the subscription.

Anyhow, the four Inns own these tracts of property. Oceans of calm in and around the City of London. Fine old buildings. Like an Oxford or Cambridge college. Ample lawns. A croquet hoop here and there. A garden party, a big white tent and a brass band. They weren't exactly the sort of place most of Keenan's clients would feel right at home in. Not quite Notting Hill, Brixton or Hackney. More the sort of place the good lady Nick would expect her son to work from. If he wasn't dead.

Keenan was expecting me. I wasn't kept waiting one minute. He even came out to greet me, shake hands, offer me coffee before we settled down. I said yes. I needed time to shake off that cloying sense of climbing back down into a cesspit I thought I'd slid out of years ago.

'So tell me about this book,' he invited as soon as he was settled safely behind his desk.

He wasn't a fool. You can carry consorting with people too far. If you didn't keep the barriers up, they might forget you were something special.

I haven't told you much about Keenan, except he was a socialist. (Whatever that meant. Time was, I thought I was. A few others did too. *Plus ça change.*)

He was from older English stock than Jack Nicholas. He could trace his ancestry back to the seventeenth century, when his great-great-great-great-etc. had been foreign secretary or something like. For several years, Keenan had been dignified with the title QC. That is to say: a senior barrister.

For all his wealth, family standing and personal confidence – born, you could say, with a psychological silver spoon in his mouth: he didn't have to spend half his life trying to find out who he was, or persuading the world or himself he really did exist – Keenan was actually a most charming man. He was difficult to fault, except for an odd, lingering impression that his interest in the working class wasn't that different from the interest his ancestors might've expressed in the family retainers.

Physically, he was unprepossessing. Short, stout, with thin metal-rimmed glasses, and a shock of hair that was already turning white. The most distinctive feature about him was: in contrast to my several, he didn't have a chin. I mean. Like. No chin at all. But a colleague who'd seen him cut himself swore it ran red, so the other thing you'd've expected wasn't true at all.

'Well, it's a book about the British left. . . Particularly, the legal left. Obviously, you can't write about the legal left in isolation from the left as a whole, but that's the focus. . .'

It sounded good. Convincing. Meaningless garbage, of course, but convincing meaningless garbage of the sort if my memory didn't fail me the left loved to spout at one another during long nights in the pub or all day Saturday arguing for control of a pathetic voluntary agency or an unknown splinter faction of a rarified political party.

He nodded wisely:

'I can see that. Why the legal left?'

'Don't you think. . . Sometimes. . . We. . .' I threw the 'we' in casually, hoping he'd ignore the rumours he was bound to have heard about my own activities over the last few years:

'We epitomize the contradictions. Working against the establishment, but within it. Dependent on it for a living, but seeking to destroy it. Fighting to protect people from its excesses, but legitimizing them.'

The words rolled off my tongue like it was only yesterday. I only wished I could remember what they meant.

I noticed that the way he held his hands while listening wasn't that different from the coroner I'd seen before the weekend. As if to spite me, he unravelled his fingers and picked up his mug of coffee, slurping from it the way I hated. I guess the guy had somehow to show he wasn't pure aristocrat.

'Who's commissioned it?'

I smiled secretively:

'I'm sorry. I've been asked not to say for the time being.'

He didn't seem to know enough about publishing to recognize the answer as pure bullshit. Nor did I.

I felt inspired. My cover was sheer brilliance. Mick Belcher couldn't't've done it. He wouldn't't've known, as I knew from years in the business, that lawyers love to talk about themselves, and that left-wingers love to talk about themselves, and that in consequence there was nothing so irresistible to a left-wing lawyer than an opportunity to talk about himself.

I leaned back in my chair. I almost didn't have to do any more. Just sit there. It would all flow. He asked me:

'I heard you'd left practice. Have you been writing since?'

'Thinking, let's say.'

I grinned openly. He was positively eating out of my hand. Making a show of interest in me. I was going to put him on paper. I was going to bring him publicity. It didn't matter how famous they already were: they always wanted more.

He wasn't, of course, to know that was why I was grinning.

'Who else have you seen?'

He made it seem like an incidental.

It was the perfect question. After my answer, I would own him:

'No one. Yet. I thought I'd start with you. . .'

It really cost him. To keep the smirk off his face.

'And where do you want to start?'

'With your chambers, I should think. After all, it was a pretty major thing to do, to set up a group the way you did. . .'

He knew what I was referring to. You probably won't. I'll explain.

Theoretically, any barrister is obliged to take any case which he is competent to do, meaning professionally competent to do. He is not supposed to reject work because he is, for example, pro-landlord or pro-employer. The idea is that his expertise should be available to anyone, no matter how mighty or how humble.

But it's a funny thing. If you're a solicitor acting for a landlord or an employer looking for a famous name to do your dirty work at a very high level of pay – maybe five figures for a day's work – you find that any barrister you want is easily available. Whereas. If you're acting for a tenant or some other jerk on fixed-rate, legal aid scales of pay, suddenly the same guy's awfully busy, terribly sorry, would love to do the case. But.

It isn't exactly news that lawyers haven't got a hard-earned reputation for working for the oppressed. Given the financial background, and the class lawyers have come from, you'd be a fool to expect anything else.

31

What Keenan did that was different from most of the rest of the bar was to set up a group, a chambers, which specialized in the problems of the poor, the victims, the disenfranchised and the dispossessed, operating, contrary to the rules, on behalf of them and them alone.

What made it even more appealing that I was sitting at his feet was that Keenan hadn't been the only one to develop ideas along these lines. There had been another such 'socialist collective of barristers,' as they liked to call themselves. Their points of distinction had been to set up their group outside the four Inns of Court, where the rest of the London bar worked, closer to their clients they claimed, but otherwise they too were selective about their clients.

They, however, went further. They actually used to share their fees, so the high earners subsidized the low. At least Keenan's group weren't that fanatical. By coming to him, I was acknowledging his priority over them.

'Well, you know, it wasn't something that just happened. . .'

He meant: I spent years thinking my way into it, organizing it, before anyone else got involved, or has to be mentioned.

I nodded sombrely, as if this was exactly what I wanted to hear. I took out my notebook. Made like I was writing notes. He wouldn't need prompting for a while.

It took the best part of an hour to get on to the history of the group itself. There were very few of them when they started. Keenan. Four other men, one woman.

I remembered some of those early people. Wishart. Red faced to the point where it looked like he was going to catch fire. Spoke like he was about to burst: staccato, rapid gunfire, too quick to keep up with. Fat Harry Matheson. The best company of all. He couldn't find clothes to cover the whole of his body all of the time. His belly flopped outside of trousers he could barely keep up.

Carrie – Caroline – Creemer. Slim. Attractive if ice

is to your taste. When she wore trousers, they were tight enough to count the pubic hairs. Soon after they started, they had been joined by Sue Cannon. Thorough. Hard-working. A little soul who drank a bit too much to cover up the strain of practising as a barrister. It didn't come as any great shock to me when she decided to switch over to being a solicitor.

'And Orbach?' I could afford a certain amount of shall we say less than friendly questioning. It was consistent with my cover.

'Russel Orbach. Yes. He was with me at the beginning. . .'

He didn't want to talk about Orbach. He was torn. He wanted to co-operate with me, he wanted to be invited to talk, to be written about. But. He didn't want to talk about Orbach.

I had no real reason to press him on the subject, save authenticity, and perhaps a chance to persuade him into wanting all the more to talk about something or someone else.

Orbach was, apart from Keenan, the best known of the founders. Aggressive, arrogant, argumentative. He was like a whole bunch of other Jewish professionals I'd known, especially lawyers.

There had been problems. Orbach had split from the group a few years after it began. Every kind of rumour flew around the movement. Not just the movement: the profession as a whole had their eyes on Keenan's chambers, and it loved to gossip.

Mostly, the rumours were, Orbach was doing too well. By the time he split, he was highly successful. What the anti-Orbach faction said was: he wanted to get out there and earn some real money. The anti-Keenans summed it up pithily: 'the politics of envy'.

'It wasn't just the founders,' Keenan bit: 'There were others.'

He reminded me that they'd been joined after a couple of years by a relatively well-known barrister. Jeffrey Jones hadn't stayed either. He had taken up politics full-time, and was one of that new breed of left-wing councillors who live on their allowances and spend their days in meetings part-time lefties only get the thrill of at night.

Also. After Jeff Jones left, there had been a gradual influx of new people. Over the next couple of years while I was still in touch, four or five new barristers and a new clerk. Until recently, I'd never thought them of much consequence. One of these, though, was Jack Nicholas.

'Didn't I hear he'd died recently?' I asked, as disingenuously as I could manage. Which didn't sound very to me. But seemed to get by him.

'Yes. He was in an accident, on his bicycle. We miss him a great deal.'

'I'm sure. I met him a few times. I think. . . Well,' I laughed, as if mildly embarrassed:

'You probably won't remember. But I and Anne. . . Godwin. . . We had a short, er, relationship. . . I think during that time, I went on a chambers' outing. . . To his house. Would that be right?'

'His parents' house. Yes. We went too.' The we wasn't royal: he meant himself and his wife.

Now he mentioned her, I remembered his wife. How could I forget? She was one of the biggest bitches I ever encountered. Rich as Croesus. And titled. The Lady Helen: she was so neurotic if Freud had to cure her, he'd never have lived long enough to do anything else.

'He was still young. . .' I had a bit of leeway before I was showing excessive interest.

'Yes.'

Funny that. I got the impression he was no keener to talk about Jackdaw than he was to talk about Orbach.

I said, as pleasantly as the substance allowed:

'You see, I can't take an uncritical approach. . .'

'Of course,' he waved a hand as if he welcomed close scrutiny.

'I just wondered how you thought you had done, in terms of. . . Shall we say cohesion?' The spectre of the left.

He shrugged:

'Orbach is the only one who left us, but continued at the bar. Doesn't that say something?'

'I don't know. It just seemed to me. . . Well, that you'd lost more than just Orbach. . .'

'What do you mean?'

I reached up to see if my head was still in place, or whether he'd snapped it off completely.

'Well, there was Sue Cannon. Jeffrey Jones. Orbach. Unless I'm mistaken, you had a couple of pupils, who didn't stay. . .'

'Mary ffoulkes? She's on television now.' Presenter on a consumer rights show. I caught it once in a while.

'No. There was another. At the beginning?'

'Bob Carter.'

'Yes.'

Keenan nodded:

'But not a good barrister. . . That was all. . . We were unlucky.'

And he was bristling. He hadn't come down off of my question: you've lost a lot of people. I couldn't quite make the connection. Yet.

'Then Jack Nicholas. . . That was different, of course. . .'

Keenan nodded, like he was miles away:

'You know about the others, of course?'

'Meaning?' I had the upper hand for the moment, and didn't mind showing it.

'Peter Wishart. . . and Carrie. . . Caroline Creemer.'

I shook my head. 'I hadn't heard they'd left.'

'No. They didn't. They died too. I thought you'd know that. Most of the group are in their thirties. Three deaths,' he scowled, bitter, as if it was personal between him and God:

'Three deaths in the last eighteen months. . . It's hard, David, I tell you it's hard. . .'

He looked straight at me, genuinely grief-stricken, though whether for the loss of personal friends, or of soldiers in his small, private army it was hard to tell.

Me? I said nothing. I was thinking. I was thinking: he's right. It is hard. And. Not a little bit odd.

Chapter Three

I remember a line from one of the early James Bond books. It went something like this:

'Once is happenstance. Twice is coincidence. Three times is enemy action.'

What do you call four?

About seven thirty, he suggested we call it a night, and go for a 'quick one.' I knew about lawyers' 'quick ones'. They were the ones that hit you hardest. You weren't expecting to get smashed. They sort of crept up on you and by the time you knew it, you were well away. I'd spent the best part of the last several years perfecting the art.

The pub he took me to was just outside the Inner Temple. The Witness Box. There were a couple of tables on the street, but the bar was downstairs. Like a dungeon. It was crowded at the time we arrived, mostly with barristers. The sound of plum hitting roof of mouth bounced off the cellar walls.

Several of his colleagues were in the pub. Mainly the younger ones, people who'd come in even after Nicholas. But Jane Daws was there, who'd joined at about that time, and whom I'd known before.

I never did quite understand what tagged her a socialist: she spent more time dressing and making up than reading the Collected Works. Every time she opened her mouth she sounded like a fishwife: high pitched shriek, everything she said was either plain stupid, or just superfluous. She wasn't bad looking, I guess, in a superficial sort of way: curly, mouse-brown hair, light eye make-up, skinny, no tits.

When we came in, Keenan was quick to explain what I was up to, and that I was interested in how come so many people had left his group. They were on their best behaviour. I don't mean actually good. The best they knew how in the circumstances. They wanted me to see them as one big happy family.

I was introduced to the others. Errol Cornell was mid-twenties, black; hanging from his shoulder was a 'personal stereo'. The things that drive you crazy on the underground. Not loud enough to listen to, but making a monotonous, tinny scratching sound that prevents you concentrating on anything else.

Then there was Gerry Gilligan. He was a tall, thin bloke, with a biker's helmet and a tarnished leather jacket at his feet. I didn't figure him for a faggot. Quite the opposite. You could smell what the women were thinking about him.

I'm talking about Jane Daws. And Marguerita Brad-kinson. If anyone could've made me want to bother again, she was it. In stark contrast to Jane, she was dressed down – sloppily, chaplinesque in baggy trousers, scuffed shoes, a jacket that was too big for her by several sizes. Also: messy long blonde hair. Nor slim. Indeed, distinctly chubby. But impish. The sort of face you could think it was worth the effort just to wake up next to. When she went to the toilet, my eyeballs went with.

The other woman was, like Cornell, black. As I recollect, when I last knew those chambers there hadn't been a black face amongst them. I guess they were in fashion, because, suddenly, there were two. I must be racist or something because I couldn't get all the way round her name. She didn't have much to say for herself. Just sat. Watching Gilligan, and Keenan. Not me.

It wasn't only the women who had the hots for Gilligan. I'd met Arthur Farquharson before. He joined the group, I guess, a year or two earlier than Anne Godwin. In those days, he was extremely suave, women rang up for him all the time, in the pub after a conference there was always one lying around in his pocket, his prematurely balding fair hair gave him a distinguished look, his face was all kindness, and he dressed like daddy's allowance was more than the rest of them had to live on.

He'd come out pretty soon after joining. His clothes had gone butch: leather jackets, designer dungarees (with a wee red loop on one side that couldn't hold a toothbrush, let alone a hammer,) thick, hob-nailed shoes. Also, a bushy moustache. If I hadn't seen him on the streets of Earl's Court just after closing time, I'd seen a thousand like him.

Keenan left us soon after he'd bought a round. It took me a little while, but wasn't difficult, to bring the subject back to Nicholas. They were willing to talk about anything I wanted. So long as it had to do with them.

Marguerita asked. All innocent eyes and joggling tits.

'Do you really think a lot of people have left? I mean, for the size of the group, and the time it's been going?'

I didn't. Before Keenan gave me the full break-down.

'Perhaps not. Not for the straight bar, anyway.' I had the key to answering all their questions. Implying they ought to be viewed somehow differently from other lawyers was enough to show I knew they were 'special'.

'But if you add the three who died,' I dropped in casually.

Gilligan was watching me closely. I had to be careful.

'Yeah. You've certainly been kind of unlucky. . .'

'Unlucky? Dropping like flies,' a voice boomed from above and behind me.

I grinned. I'd know that voice anywhere:

'Fat Harry. . .'

'To the last pound. . .' He grabbed a stool from a neighbouring table and stuck it halfway up his back-side:

'How are you? We haven't seen you around here for a long time. I thought you'd quit practice? Did you bring me a brief?'

38

I laughed. He had that effect on me. Anything he said could make me laugh.

The conversation came back to the less voluntary deserters. I was interested in them all, and had to remind myself that it was Jack Nicholas for whom I was being paid to find a palatable epitaph.

'I heard he'd been drinking a lot the night it happened. . .'

I spoke offhandedly. Like throwing a dart straight into someone's eye. You could hear a corpse fart.

'We don't talk about it much,' Harry said firmly. He was the most senior member present, and not afraid to remind them:

'We miss him a lot. We were all very fond of him. . .'

I don't like it when people lie to me. This was a group of fifteen to twenty barristers. And socialists. There wasn't a cat's chance in hell that they were 'all' fond, let alone 'very fond', of him.

Gilligan got me out of Harry's corner.

'He hadn't had that much to drink. . . None of us had.'

Harry frowned at him. The others looked embarrassed.

For a moment, it looked as if the party was going to break up. Fat Harry got up to leave, which took care of half the bodyweight in the pub. Art Farquharson, too, after one, last, lingering, eyeball caress of Gilligan's lanky limbs (a video he'd play back in slow motion later, when he had the appropriate equipment to hand), headed for the wilds of my part of town. The black woman had children to attend to. Errol followed her out.

That left Gilligan, Marguerita Bradkinson and Jane Daws. And me.

I had to get things moving. Desperate, I went to an extreme:

'Anyone want another drink?'

That's another thing about lawyers. They're all mean. They never say no. The round cost me the best part of three quid. I wrote down a fiver for expenses.

'How did you get on with Alex?' Jane asked, bright green.

'He has a lot to say. . .' I grinned, to let them know I was an ally.

You'd never hear a word against him, though. Their relationship with him was positively umbilical. It was all between the lines. He had such a great reputation, he had been around so long, they could never hope to catch up. It gave them security. But. At a price. Forever the shadows.

'He represented the Nicholas family at the inquest, didn't he?'

Gilligan's eyes narrowed. He was beginning to wonder what time I was keeping.

'It was a gesture. For the family. We were genuinely upset, you know.' Like I said. Every word she spoke was superfluous.

'I'm not surprised,' I said mildly:

'If you take the people who've gone off somewhere else, and the people who've died, that's quite a chunk of the group you've managed to lose. . .'

Gilligan to Bradkinson: quick look. I took a shot in the dark:

'Why did Orbach leave?'

It was a fair question. For my cover. But my interest was about as genuine as their grief over Jackdaw.

'Before our time,' Marguerita said, sucking Gilligan up into her answer.

All eyes were on the Daws.

She flushed:

'You know we don't talk about it,' she told the others.

'Hey, what's the big deal?' Somehow I managed to convey: if we don't talk about what I want to talk about, we don't talk.

Gilligan said:

'"'Twas in a foreign country and besides the wench is dead. . ."'

'But who was the wench?'

I told you there'd been a lot of rumours at the time Orbach left. I also said most of them had been about

40

money and professional jealousy. I should've added. Inevitably, the song of sex could also be heard in the not too distant background.

Jane Daws got up to go to the toilet. My eyes stayed behind.

'Tell me about the others. . .Wishart and Creemer.'

'Pete died. . .Oh, about eighteen months ago. It was in Germany. He was there for a conference. You know he was very involved in Germany?'

I had a vague recollection. From years before. Soon after they started up as a chambers. He'd been peripherally involved, providing support – theoretical, moral, political, maybe legal, not actual or practical – to one of those German revolutionary groups which followed Baader–Meinhof. They had a name like: Red September, February 29th, White Christmas.

'Wasn't Orbach involved in that too?'

'The first I heard,' Gilligan answered.

My information was all out of date, from before they were born as barristers.

'What happened?'

'There was a fire. In the house where he was staying. It was pretty grisly.'

'We do seem. . . We do seem to meet violent ends. . .' Marguerita was genuinely frightened.

Gilligan reassured her:

'If people are going to die, at our ages, the odds are it won't be peacefully in bed.'

If that was his idea of comfort, I'd like to hear how he put the frighteners on. Marguerita had gone completely white. As Daws returned from the lavatory, she got up for them to leave together. Without Gilligan.

He watched me watch Marguerita leave.

'I thought you'd be going with her. . .' I said.

'Nah. I've been. There's some places you don't want to go back to. You know?'

I knew. But I wouldn't mind finding out for myself.

There was just him and me.

'And Carrie? Did she meet a . . . violent end too?'

41

'Yup.'

I waited.

He didn't tell.

I could've asked. I could've bought him a drink.

I did neither:

'I guess I'll see you again. I'll be around for a bit.'

He grinned:

'Maybe.'

'Meaning?'

'Meaning like you've said, people don't seem to last long around here. I might not still be here.'

He didn't give a damn.

I decided. I liked him. He was a real A1 shit stirrer. And. Stirred shit was what the doctor had ordered.

I'd picked up enough to think about. The question was: where now? I knew what Captain Furillo would do. He'd leave it over for a week. Till the next episode. I couldn't give it a week. But. I could give myself a night to sleep on it.

Sleep's a good sorter. You burn up what don't matter and wash off the rest to see it good and clear. When I woke, Jack Nicholas was light years away. The things that mattered were: the split with Orbach; and all those advocates appearing before the highest court of them all.

I had no in to Orbach, except the same cover I'd used on Keenan. From what I remembered, Orbach was about ten times as smart and therefore ten times as likely to see through it. I did have another in that seemed worth a try.

One of the people who'd left the group was Sue Cannon. To become a solicitor. Remember? She was part of that small minority I'd kept in touch with from the old days. Vaguely. She'd always been kind to me. Given me as much work as I wanted. As a matter of fact, though I hate to admit it of any lawyer, she was one of the kinder people I ever knew.

Of course, she had her faults. They used to call her the drain. Because she could pour it away. Or the mouth. For obvious reasons. (I mean: she talked a lot. Not the other. So far as I knew.)

I got my interview with her by shock tactics. Rang up. Offered to buy her a meal. I even took her somewhere good. M'sieur Frog on the Essex Road. Her end of town. A lot of people seemed to have moved up that way. Only I was still stuck in bedsit bogland.

It was quite a few days before we met. I hadn't actually seen her for two or more years. Our transactions were always on the 'phone. She was there before me. So much for the joys of public transport. She waved at me from behind our table and her spectacles. She looked good.

'Hey. You lost weight.'

Her size of person (midget) couldn't carry spare.

'Yup.'

I glanced down at the ashtray:

'Ah. . .'

I remembered when she'd quit. She'd undergone hypnosis to walk away from forty a day. That was when she started to put on weight. Switched from jeans to loose dresses.

'Nothing I like to see so much as someone fallen off the wagon. . .'

She held a pack out to me. I shook my head:

'Uhuh. Smoke my own.'

Camel. And Southern Comfort. When I could afford them. Which was now.

The owner came over:

'Hallo. Haven't seen you for a long time. Shall I explain the blackboard?'

We both ordered. Sue took a special: a fancy, baked salmon. I was into as many steaks as I could put down to expenses. While it lasted.

'Wine?'

'Sue? Still drinking?' As if it could be in doubt.

She·stuck her tongue out at me.

'Well? You're eating fish. . .'

This was why I like Sue. Straight to the point:

'A bottle of house white for me. And a bottle of house

43

red for him.'

It took to when we were considering whether to order another bottle each, or just the one more between us, to get the conversation around to Keenan's chambers.

'D'you ever regret quitting?'

'No. Certainly not.' She wasn't lying.

'D'you see much of them?'

'I brief one or two of them. That's all.'

'I guess. . . You wouldn't really have any close friends left there. . . Not since Carrie. . .'

There were times when I appreciated my delicacy almost as much as my intellect.

She frowned:

'We weren't that close, you know. Not after I left.'

'I always thought. . .' It was feigned surprise, but genuine.

'You know how it is when you belong to these groups . . . When you leave, suddenly it's gone, you've become a non-person. With us or agin' us.'

'I never belonged to one. . .' Or anything else. But I had a faint idea what she was talking about.

'Why'd'you leave, Sue? You never really told me. . .'

'Oh, I don't know. It all seems so long ago now.'

We settled for a further bottle each.

'Things changed. As people joined. It wasn't the same as when it started. It was exciting at the beginning. New. Adventurous. We were like a family, or a team. It was personal, and the theory was that bit less important. We trusted each other, and each other's instincts. Later, it became all theory, no feeling, for each other or anyone else. I began to get sick of it. . .

'It's not very easy to explain. I'm a socialist, a believer,' she laughed, 'But I'm a realist. When we had a lot of people, a lot of theoretical chatter, everyone was trying to be leftier than thou. . . Left-wing one-upmanship. There's always a yet more radical posture. It made me feel, well, there was lot of hypocrisy. . . People, some of them with private money – actual or in anticipation – or good practices, making a living off the backs of the poor, and translating themselves into their saviours. . . You must know the sort of thing I mean?'

'Me. I got out.' But what she was saying put into words many of the reasons I'd quit.

'It's difficult to remember the examples now. Ireland. That's always a good one. Justifying the violence, oh, not supporting it, of course,' she ladled sarcasm all over the last two words, 'but explaining it. But, you know, they didn't have to live with it, and, well, some of the violence has been pretty extreme, pretty inhumane, unjustifiable on any terms. . .

'But that's just an example. You got the same sort of attitude towards anywhere else in the world. . . Anywhere except England, of course. Like India and Pakistan, Germany, the Middle East. . .'

'How'd Orbach feel about that?' The Middle East. Israel. As a Jew, I knew I had mixed feelings.

She shrugged:

'I don't suppose any of them stopped to ask themselves. You weren't supposed to have feelings, just theories. . .'

'Was that why he left?'

She shook her head:

'I don't think so. It may have been part of it. . . Alienation. . . I certainly felt that. . .'

'Orbach,' I prompted:

'What actually happened? I never found out. . .'

'Me neither. They were pretty close-mouthed about it. . . I know there was talk of legal action, by him. . . Against them. . . But I don't know for what. . . I caught some of the rumours. . . I should think you did too. . .'

'It was all about money, wasn't it?' Meaning it wasn't.

'There was a rumour. . . Nothing more than that. . . That he'd been having a scene with Helen. . . Helen Keenan. . .'

I laughed out loud:

'She was ten years older than him!'

'So?'

I had displeased her.

45

She was getting to an age when there were people she fancied who were ten years younger than her.

I shrugged:

'I don't know. I remember Orbach. And her. I went on a weekend in Wiltshire – chambers' outing – where she was. That was after he'd left, of course. But. I wouldn't have thought. . .'

She shrugged too:

'I don't know. That was what I heard. I couldn't find out more. . .'

She was admitting she'd tried.

The owner hovered over us.

We discussed dessert and more wine for a few minutes. We used the break to visit, in turn, the toilets. I worked at a couple of French cartoons on the wall to see if I'd forgotten everything I'd learned in school. I had.

Once we were both sitting again, and the hardest part of breaking up meringue chantilly was over, I asked her what I really wanted to know.

'Tell me about Caroline? What did happen to her?'

She shuddered.

'I don't know all the details. I got it all second-hand. From the papers or from the group. But. . . What I heard was that she was with this guy. . . A black man. . . Not quite living with him. . . But seeing him a lot. . . They had a row. . .'

She really didn't want to describe it. She wasn't putting on a show. I wanted to hear. I had to ask:

'Go on. . .'

'There were a lot of people. . . Who said. . . It was a heavy relationship . . . I mean. . . Very emotional. . . Maybe violent. . . He. . . Well, I don't know. . . I mean. . . Didn't you read about it? It was all over the papers at the time!'

'I. . . Well, I haven't been reading the papers for a while. . .' Anyhow, not the stories with a lot of words in them.

'Oh, hell. He killed her. That's what they said and that's what it looked like. He had gone, gotten out, out

46

of the country, back to Ghana. . . By the time she was found. . . In her flat. . . Did you ever go there? I did. Lots of times. That made it worse. I could see it. In her living-room. That's where they found her. Stabbed.'

She looked down at her wine. They'd already cleared away the dessert plates. I couldn't figure why she wouldn't look at me for a while. Then I saw the tears. Dropping slowly from her eyes. Two by two. At a steadily increasing pace. Who'd've thought it?

Eventually she looked up. She didn't bother to hide her tears. There wasn't much point. She finished off the story:

'She'd been stabbed eighteen times. I heard. . . Her parents had her cremated. . .'

She meant: it wasn't something to have stuffed and mounted over the mantelpiece.

She offered to drive me home. The amount she'd drunk, I figured the odds in favour of the tube.

I got on at the Angel, changed at King's Cross and walked home from Gloucester Road, instead of Earl's Court.

If I hadn't, I doubt I would've noticed I was being followed. Guys walking behind you down the Earl's Court Road late at night aren't news. When they don't bother, you might as well start hiding the mirror.

I played the usual games. Down Bina Gardens, turned left instead of right on the Old Brompton, back up Gloucester, right at Stanhope, all the way down through Harrington Gardens till I came out opposite the South Kensington station and cut through the arcade. He was waiting for me across the road, on the other side.

It was still possible I was a damned sight prettier than I was used to thinking. I crossed over, passed real close, gave him the bold eye of invitation, walked on and turned ostentatiously back to show I wanted him to follow. I was close enough when I looked around to see the sneer on his lips that told me it wasn't my arse he was after.

I'd never been tailed before. I knew one idea was to shake him. I just didn't know how. The other thing to do is tuck yourself out of sight, jump him, grab him, throw him up against a wall, slap his face every which way but straight and beat out of him the name of his boss. Oh, yeah. There's a third thing you can do. Get home as fast as your legs can carry you, and make damned sure you double lock the door.

The phone was ringing as I came in, out of breath. The voice at the other end was garbled.

'Say it again,' I ordered.

'I said, Art Farquharson was killed last night.'

My caller was Gilligan. He was drunk. Dead drunk.

'How? When? Where? Tell me what you know.'

I hadn't missed the point: killed, not died.

'I don't know much. I only heard this afternoon. Was in court. When I got back. . . Everyone knew. . .'

'Tell me.'

'Not much to tell. He was found in the street. In Earl's Court. That's where you live, isn't it?'

I didn't rise to the innuendo.

'Do you know exactly where?'

'Coleherne Road. I remember the name. He used to mention a pub called the Coleherne. Where his cottaging clientele hung out.'

Cottaging = public lavatory pick-ups = police set-ups = criminal charges.

I knew both. The pub, and the road. They were gay centres. Coleherne Road and the streets off it were where those who hadn't scored some company before closing time hung about to try their luck later.

They were about a minute away from where I stood, listening to what Gilligan had to tell me. And that would be on crutches.

I began to sweat. The combination was claustrophobic. The physical nearness of the death. My involvement with those chambers.

Gilligan told me a bit more. I could have guessed some of it. Farquharson's body was a mess. Either he didn't have the details, or he couldn't bring himself to tell me. I didn't particularly want to hear. I'd got the general picture.

He had died in the early hours of the morning. The body hadn't been found till seven o clock. The possibilities were wide open. Killed on the street. But no one who hung around Coleherne Road in the wee hours of the morning would have wanted anyone else to know that was where they street-walked. Or killed somewhere else, and dropped where maybe the killer figured Farquharson'd feel most at home.

Neither of us spoke for a while.

Eventually, I asked the question I should've asked at the beginning:

'Why're you telling me?'

He laughed loudly:

'Didn't you want to know, Mr Woolf?'

'That's a Jewish habit, answering a question with a question. Gilligan don't sound Jewish to me?'

'Doesn't it?' He answered a question with a question. And hung up.

It took me the full minute to walk there. My tail took about six seconds longer. The spot was marked in two inanimate ways. It was roped off, between portable uprights. And. A uniformed policeman stood guard. I'd never seen Coleherne Road so deserted at that time of the night. Maybe the copper wasn't cute enough.

I walked past on the other side of the street. Crossed over at the top, opposite the Coleherne pub, and turned right. My tail would be getting giddy: we were going back the way I'd galloped home before the call.

I wasn't in a hurry this time. It was just before half past twelve. Still early. It took me a few minutes to find exactly where I wanted. A dim light in a smoked-glass shop window, with no markings outside. The door looked equally uninviting.

I rapped hard enough to hurt my knuckles. The door opened about a millimetre. One of the gorillas Lewis keeps around like barristers have clerks glowered out at me. Fortunately, he recognized me. He oughta. He'd been a most welcome visitor in my home. Discussing my family. And my welfare. And my debts.

He swung the door back silently. I always figured he had a hard time with words. I checked he wasn't planning to communicate with me the way he was most at ease. He kept his arms at his side. But his fists were clenched.

'Lewis here?' I asked chirpily, as if he might just be hanging around on the off-chance I dropped in. A bit of bone in the middle of his jaw disappeared inside his chins. I think it was his idea of affirmative.

I tripped up the stairs. I wasn't afraid any more. Light-headed. Like I was stoned.

'Sit down, David. It's nice to see you. Very nice.'

He spoke soft. Like he'd heard the Corleones do in the Godfather movies. Like someone had maybe told him refined gentlemen do.

He was dressed cute, too. A light, pale blue suit, of a hue that had not become modish until recently, but cut like a thirties gangster. If I was into tie-knots, I'd wonder where he found the one that brought it out, high and firm, before it fell back in to his waistcoat. It had the same effect of making him look slender like a woman's tits can have on her waistline.

'Would you like a drink, David? What would you like to drink?' He could not have been more solicitous. That was community work for you.

He held up his glass. Suggestion.

'What is it?'

'Kir royale.'

I knew what that was. Champagne I couldn't afford. With French alcoholic Ribena I couldn't stand.

Besides, though light-headed, I wasn't exactly celebratory.

'S'Comfort?'

'Sure, David, whatever.'

He was the first person ever to recognize my personal abbreviation for the peach-based liquor which was one of the few original American alcoholic beverages to have gotten beyond the stills.

He snapped his fingers.

I sighed. I'd spent half three-score-and-ten years trying to learn how to do that. All I got was sore finger tips, and a tiny, brushing sound like I was trying to mimmick a personal stereo at a distance.

'Large?'

'Leave the bottle. . .'

The bunny reject suppressed a grin, and did as she was bid. She must have thought I was one of Lewis' closest. I got to him though: in just a fraction of second, a frown crossed his face.

'Ice?' Rabbitty asked.

I shook my head, poured my own, and threw it down my throat like I hoped it would be the last job I ever had to finish.

'There's something on your mind, David. . .'

'Yup. There's something on my mind.'

'You want to tell me about it?'

He coulda made it as a psychoanalyst if he hadn't got so many fuck-ups of his own.

'Last night. A queer got killed on Coleherne.'

'A lot of young men. . . Of this persuasion. . . Die. . . Their games can tend to get a little rough. . .'

Then he waited for me to go on.

'This one. . .was a barrister. . .'

He nodded. He knew.

'That makes it sort of news, don't you think?'

He shrugged:

'Perhaps. Is he. . . Was he a matter of concern to you?'

That was delicate. 'A matter of concern.' It could mean what I let it mean. Lewis knew I was legal. By qualification. And para-legal. By so-called employment. His question could mean: professional relations. He'd never worked me out sexually. It could've meant something else.

I dignified his discretion:

'Yeah. Professionally. I've known him a few years. We had a bit to do with one another recently. As a matter of fact, I saw him about ten days ago.'

'A friend, then?'

If he was going to help me, he was entitled to know why:

'No. I was. . . Interested in him.'

I helped myself to another wine-size shot of Southern Comfort.

He might've spent years practising to sound like a gentleman, but he couldn't help himself:

'Did you say. . . You were paying for that?'

I grinned:

'Nope.'

I felt cocky:

'Some day, Lewis, you'll call it in. . .' The favour.

He sighed, as if I might single-handedly bankrupt him:

'I always liked you, David. Even when we. . . had our little difference . . . That was business. . . Just business. . . I couldn't, you understand, I couldn't handle it any other way. . . But. . . That is why I like you. . . Because I knew, I could feel,' he lowered his voice, and yet somehow managed to emphasize the last word:

'I could feel you understood. . . That it wasn't. . .' He thrashed around for another word, but that which is born of cliché must die as cliché:

'Personal. . .'

'Sure, Lewis. . .'

God only knew where I'd found my confidence. I felt like I was twenty-five, and had just won my first big case as a qualified solicitor.

He thought for a moment. Decided I was right. He didn't mind being into me for a favour.

'I can't tell you much. His name was Farquharson, but of course you know that,' he corrected himself. It took him time to recall he was dealing with someone who wasn't a complete ape.

'It didn't happen where he was found. He was brought there. No number. No make. The boy who saw isn't too fond of the butch pastimes. . .' Like cars.

'Will you give me his name?'

Lewis shook his head. His boys belonged to him. Body and name.

'Anything else?'

'You know what sort of state he was in?'

'No. I didn't cop the news.'

He laughed. To make up for his earlier ill-grace, he reached over and refreshed my glass.

'They're not telling it on the news. . .'

I waited. My stomach didn't. It was already churning. As if it already knew.

He leaned towards me, and dropped his voice, to a whisper. Not, I should say, out of secrecy. Nor another bout of delicacy. More like a treat too good to share:

'Double-barrelled, up his. . .' He didn't need to finish. I was already there. So was a third of a bottle of Southern Comfort. In my mouth.

When I got back from the bog, Lewis had been joined by a face I didn't know.

He grinned when he saw me. Held out a hand in welcome.

'Meet my solicitor. Mr Woolf. This is Detective Sergeant Dowell. An old friend. An old friend indeed.'

'I've got to go, Lewis. Nice to meet you, Sergeant. Speak to you again?' I shot at Lewis as I raced myself to the door.

'I'm sure. I'm sure.' I heard him answer me.

I stopped running about two and half inches from the steps to my flat. Leaned against the railings to gather my breath. Fought the thought off. Not very successfully. That, I thought, was stupid.

Chapter Four

I got through what was left of the night without an invasion by armed police. Nor were they waiting for me outside my door when I emerged shortly after midday. Nor, so far as I could tell, was anyone following me when I made my way up to the corner shop to buy the papers.

Lewis wasn't right about everything. The papers had got it. In full. They were happy to use it.

I was spoiled for choice.

The Times. 'Police are still investigating the death in Earl's Court on Wednesday night or Thursday morning of Mr Arthur Farquharson, a barrister. . .'

The Sun. 'Barrister Art Farquharson's death in a sleazy street haunted by homosexuals is still puzzling police. . .'

The Guardian. 'Thir hav ben know furth devments in th allegedly French Prime Minister insisted that his homolexusal murdr. . .'

The Star. 'ADVOCATE'S ANAL ENDING.'

The moment of light-headedness which had carried me to my community worker's command centre had vanished. It was replaced with another, much more familiar, feeling. Not to put too fine a point on it, I was scared shitless. Someone out there was into death, in a heavy way. I was supposed to be finding out who. You know what killers do to people who find out what they're up to. Before you can talk to anyone else. Ugh.

With mixed intentions, I rang the Nicholas residence. His holiness answered.

'Is Mrs Nicholas available?' I asked in my snottiest tone of voice.

'Who is this, please?'

'This is the furniture department at Harrods. . .'

'Oh, just a moment, please.'

I figured them for the perfect couple. Her with her thank-yous; him all pleases.

'Mrs Nicholas? Mr Woolf, furniture department at Harrods. . .'

'Yes, Mr Woolf. . .' she dropped her voice:

'The Reverend Nicholas has gone into his study. Did you want to see me?'

We had arranged this 'call-sign' at our initial interview.

'Yes. . . Please.' The word didn't taste as bad as I had expected.

'Can you tell me. . . Do you have some news?'

Did I have some news? Sure. Me and every newspaper in the country. I figured she hadn't hit them yet.

I got out of telling her. With a bit of luck, she'd've heard for herself, before I met her. We made a date for the next day, Friday. Same place. Same time. It was acquiring the air of an affair.

I had twenty-four hours to make up my mind. There was quite a lot of me inclined to – if you'll forgive the pun – jack it in then and there, tell Mrs Reverend I wasn't her man, even give her the money back if she asked politely.

On the other hand, I'd be lying through my eye-teeth if I denied I was excited. There was another feeling. Obscure. That took me most of the day to dig out of the recesses of my underused conscience. Something about an obligation to see it through.

There'd been about a year between the first two deaths. Approximately six months again to the next. Farquharson had followed after only two more. It was too much like the sort of coincidence I didn't believe in to think it had nothing to do with the fact I was around and asking questions. Like I said, put the pressure on and hope the needle pops out of the haystack. It wasn't way outside the realms of possibility it was me that had pooped the pimple that was Art.

I spent the rest of the day doing a little research. I wanted to know more about the Creemer killing. As with Farquharson, the papers said a great deal, but told me nothing I didn't know. Wishart was harder work. He hadn't attracted a lot of attention in life; likewise in death. I finally found a paragraph in the Guardian, which, once the print had been unscrambled, suggested he had probably died twenty-four or forty-eight hours before the story appeared. Good times must've flown. It was closer to two years than the eighteen months I'd been told.

It seemed to me obvious that I was now investigating the methodical despatch of a barrister's chambers.

There are two aspects of this I found faintly confusing. First, albeit of lesser importance, was the fact that anyone could conceivably consider barristers worth killing. Secondly, the fact that the investigator was I. I brushed these irrelevancies aside, and settled down to study.

The difficulty with the thesis was the way Carrie Creemer had died. With the others, what was known was nothing. That left me free to believe what I wanted. Anything could be true. But from the newspaper accounts, and the little Sue Cannon had added before we separated at M'sieur Frog's, there was nothing at all to connect Creemer's man to her chambers.

Of course, we didn't actually know he had done it. It didn't need him to have fled the country for it to have looked that way. Given cops' attitude to blacks – and especially those with the nerve to poke around inside a palefaced pussy – he was like as not to have been charged even if he'd made the call that brought them in. If he had come back, and found her the way the papers described, he would have every reason to fear the consequences, and might just lack that unshakeable faith in British justice that could have led someone else to the nearest 999.

If I put Creemer's death on one side of the line, and her colleagues – sorry, comrades – on the other, the way it weighed up didn't balance. Ignore Creemer. Consider Wishart. Nicholas. Farquharson. They added up – in James Bond's terms – to enemy action. Look across the line at Creemer. Without the possibility that her boyfriend was innocent, it would still hardly change the dip of the scales. With that possibility, I was amply justified in what I believed.

My only job the next morning was to get hold of Anne Godwin. She was in court first thing and I didn't catch her until just before I had to go and see my client.

Somehow, I got the idea I wasn't exactly the burning desire she'd returned from holiday dying to fulfil.

'Dave?'

'Yeah. Dave Woolf. . .'

'I know.'

She wasn't questioning who I was. Just why.

I figured they'd had enough to talk about in chambers, since she'd been back, that no one had told her about my arrival on the scene.

Wrong again.

'Alex mentioned you'd been in to see him. . . Why do you want to see me?'

'Well, ain't that a warm welcome,' I muttered, mildly mortified.

'Well, OK, I suppose so, if you really want to. . .'

Gee. Thanks.

It wouldn't be until after the weekend that she could fit me in, though.

Beggars can't be choosers.

I was so late, I not only took a taxi, but even forgot to write down the fare.

Mrs Nick took her usual time getting down to business:

'What have you found out, Mr Woolf?'

'Hadn't you better sit down first?' I helped her off with her coat, placed her hat on the vacant chair, and showed her how it was done.

I had already ordered tea. I wouldn't answer until she had drunk half a cup. After all, it was her money.

'Now. Tell me.'

I don't know why. You can't explain this sort of thing. She wasn't just a client any more. But a frail, middle-aged woman, whom I liked and wanted to help. I felt. . . I don't know. Filial?

'I've. . . You've read the papers?'

I had hoped that between yesterday's call, and today's meeting, she would've got halfway there.

I could remember a similar sort of sensation when I was in practice.

I'd be really tied up in someone's case. Writing letters. Making calls. Negotiating a good deal.

Then they'd come to see me. I'd be bubbling with success. They couldn't understand. They thought I was selling them out. They hadn't been into the dark corners of their own cases, like I had. Nor heard what the other side had to say. They hadn't gone through the tunnel I was being paid to find the end of for them. They couldn't appreciate the light when they saw it.

She shook her head slowly:

'My husband sees the papers. He's usually a day or two behind. I don't read them until he's finished. We don't. . . He doesn't. . . We don't,' I was relieved she'd decided who she was talking about:

'We don't pay a lot of attention to worldly matters.'

She meant: he doesn't.

'I'm sorry. There's been. . . Another death. . .'

She understood immediately what I meant. In those chambers. She went as ghoulishly white as her hair was blue-rinsed. I pushed her cup and saucer towards her. I almost pushed her the plate of cream cakes too but I guessed it wasn't that good an idea and stopped myself in time.

I told her what I knew. I edited it. I told her there had been four deaths. Until the day before yesterday, there were only three. I admitted I might have been ready to ascribe three to a lousy run of luck. Wishart and her son seemed accidental. Creemer had certainly been murdered, and the finger pointed at an untraceable African.

'Three deaths. . .' She had managed to forget the fourth:

'But they're so young. . .'

She was going the direction I'd followed.

I told her what, after all, were the only two solid points of information about her own son:

'The accident was suspicious, or ought to have caused suspicion. That is correct. Your impression that no one cared, including his colleagues, would also seem to be correct. But. . . Well, I have no idea yet why Keenan wasn't anxious to turn the inquest into a search for something more. . .'

'Thank you.' She had heard nothing new. Unless that she was right came as a surprise.

There was a cupful of silence.

'You. . . You don't believe my son's death was an accident, then?' She returned to my company.

I shrugged:

'I don't know, Mrs Nicholas. I don't know,' I emphasized the last word:

'But, no, to use your word, I don't believe it. Wishart? Well, accidents do happen. Creemer? People get killed. . .'

'You haven't told me,' she reminded me softly I still hadn't filled her in on Farquharson.

'And I'm not going to.'

The sun must've burst into the room, because my face felt hot and flushed.

'But. . . It wasn't an accident?'

'No, ma'am. It wasn't an accident. I'd say. Closer to the Creemer killing.'

She was taut with tension. Her first instinct was predictable:

'You must go to the police, Mr Woolf. You must tell them what you know.'

'What do I know, Mrs Nicholas? Nothing. Precisely nothing. Two accidents. Two murders. They must know that much for themselves, already.'

'But it's a matter for them. Wouldn't you agree?'

It's a funny thing. But. I could swear she was playing devil's advocate. Manoeuvring me into saying:

'I'm not sure.'

'Why?'

Not: of course you must go to the police, Mr Woolf; how could you think of doing anything else; you must leave it to the experts; they'll know what to do. Why? It was my job to give voice to her instincts.

I didn't answer her at once. I hailed the waiter. Tea. Hot. Lots of it. There's an idea about to be born. I waited till after it had arrived, and even until after it had been allowed time to mash. She poured.

'Just suppose. . . Suppose I'm right that what we're looking at is. . . Well, some sort of vendetta against your son's chambers. . .

'And. Go to the other thing. I said Keenan wasn't pushing the coroner into a corner. Now maybe that's innocent. Maybe, just maybe, he was trying to minimize publicity, pain, and so on. . .'

She waved her hand impatiently. That wasn't it.

'All right. If that wasn't it. Then why? Then whatever it's about is something known, at least to Keenan, possibly others in the chambers . . .'

I should have paused at, instead of brushing aside, the question: why would anyone think barristers worth killing?

She digested my reasoning with as much struggle as if I'd tried to get her to eat a hearty meal laid out on her son's coffin. But she was no slouch. It didn't take her too long to get there:

'Whatever that would be. . . Would be something Jack knew about?'

'Maybe. If not knew about, was involved in.'

'I don't think, Mr Woolf, you knew my son very well. He would never. . . He was never. . . He could never be involved in anything. . . Anything . . .'

She couldn't finish the sentence, so I did it for her:

'Anything shameful? I don't know, Mrs Nicholas. I'm not saying he was. But. You hung in there while

60

I spelled it out for you. And. We both got to the same place. Maybe. . . Maybe what you or I might not consider shameful, he would. Who knows? Do you think. . . Are you sure you knew him that well?'

I was taking a risk. Of upsetting her. You don't make omelettes.

I stopped thinking.

Time stood still.

I don't think I have ever. I mean ever in my entire life. Met anyone. So stupid. As me.

'Mr Woolf? Mr Woolf? Are you all right?'

I nodded slowly. All right. But not all there.

'Have you got a diary, Mrs Nicholas?'

'Yes. Of course. . .'

She fished a Protestant Page-A-Day from her handbag:

'Here. . .'

It was my turn. I tried the other words:

'Thank you.'

From the inside jacket of my pocket, I took the notes I'd made the night before. I didn't really need to bother. I knew what I would find anyway.

'They had a meeting. . . A chambers' meeting. . . Once a month. . . On the last. . .'

'The last Wednesday. I know. Whenever we were arranging to see them, it was the one permanent commitment. . .'

I pointed to the dates on my notes. And then to the dates on the page of her diary which had last year, this year and next set out at a glance.

'No. I don't understand. . . Oh, wait a minute. Oh. . . Oh. . .'

For a second, I thought she was going to faint. Until that moment, we were talking suspicion. Perhaps strong suspicion. Perhaps probability. From then on we were talking proof positive. Each of the deaths had taken place on the last Wednesday of a month.

'Don't you think. . . That. . . That's enough to go to the police with?'

I shrugged:

61

'Maybe. Yes. Sure. I can go to the police. I can tell them what I know. Then. They take over. OK? Is that enough for you?'

Logically, she ought to say: yes, do that. That was what her life's experience should have dictated. This was not about her life. It was about her son's death:

'What would Jack have done?' I asked softly, gently, as only the hand with a full house of aces can do.

She nodded slowly. Her son was a socialist. In a barristers' chambers. He trusted the police about as far as Lewis did. Or me. I was gambling. Some of it might have rubbed off on his mother.

'I. . . I don't agree with him. . . I don't think he was right. . . But. . .'

Jackdaw's politically assumed hatred of the police coincided with what she wanted. She couldn't have spelled out why. A dash of faith in Jack. A gut feeling if the police got their hands on it, it would turn out wrong, or not turn out at all. A light seasoning of she wanted to keep control of it.

We talked money before we split. I'd long run over the payment on account. She didn't flinch when I asked for the same again. Wrote a cheque out. And paid for the tea. As she rose, she smiled:

'That's not all you've cost me today, Mr Woolf. . .'

I raised my eyebrows in question.

'Couldn't you have thought of a department other than furniture? Where I could have bought something small?'

I laughed as she left.

I was still laughing as I noticed a familiar face rise from a table by the door, and follow her out.

Then I stopped laughing.

We wove our way through the store, like a New Year's Eve dancing snake by relatives who couldn't bear to touch one another. Mrs Nicholas. My unfruitful fan from the night before. Me.

In furniture, he and I hesitated. He wanted a good position to watch from and catch her exit. I couldn't locate myself until he had.

62

The lady didn't linger long. I grinned as she gazed at a group of dining-room chairs. She was checking prices, observing details, preparing her explanation of why she had changed her mind about a purchase.

Outside, the doorman hailed a cab for her. Gimbo hovered nearby, to catch her destination. Then, nonchalantly, uninterested, he walked down to Hans Place, where he was parked. As he crumpled and threw into the gutter the ticket stuck on his windscreen, he turned and saw me watching. He made no attempt to hide from me; stared straight at me; grinned. As I approached him, he climbed into his car and drove away without another glance.

I wandered slowly back to my flat. Stopped for a drink at the Drayton Arms. Settled into a corner from where I could see both entries to the bar. Waited as long as it took me to read the London Standard from cover to cover – ten minutes, and that included the stock market prices. Then, home.

The light was on in my flat. The safety lock wasn't. I'd been burgled till there wasn't anything left worth stealing. I was more scared there'd still be someone inside.

'I hope you don't mind,' the Detective Sergeant held up a glass.

'If you've finished it, I will. . .'

'Not at all. I brought a bottle.' He gestured to the mantelpiece.

He had too.

'I was right, wasn't I?'

'S'Comfort? Sure. Shall I help myself?'

'It's your flat. . .'

'Uh. Right. Which sort of reminds me. . .'

He shook his head:

'Warrant? Nah. Never believed in them. You don't need them if you've got grounds to suspect a crime in progress.'

'And you've always got those?'

He laughed and finished off what was in his glass:

'If I haven't when I go in, I usually have by the time I leave.'

He was like a weasel. I felt I ought to get out a tape-measure. Check he was regulation minimum height. But it was his head that was small, and sharp, not his body. I decided maybe not to get too fresh.

'D'you build this?'

The table he was sitting at. I nodded. I'd built the bed-platform beneath which it nestled, too. Long ago. When I first moved in. When I'd been broke enough to have to let out the back room. When the last of the lodgers left, I'd stayed in the front room: living, eating, sleeping. Used the back room for spare, or for work. Even when I'd gone back to being broke, I'd never relet it. There never was a contest between food, and avoiding human contact.

I sat down opposite him, and pushed his bottle over. He poured himself another shot. If it'd been full when he arrived, one thing he did well was to hold his liquor.

'I've been checking up on you, Mr Woolf. . .'

'Surprise, surprise.'

'You don't have a practice certificate, do you?'

'Uh. Practising certificate? Right. I've heard of them . . . They're, well, sort of expensive. . .'

Checking up on people was something else he obviously did well.

'But illegal to practise without. . . So if our mutual friend . . .' Lewis.

'. . .Calls you his solicitor, I got to draw one of two conclusions. He's a liar or you are practising illegally. Which one would you go for, Mr Woolf?'

'Well, I guess that would depend. . .'

'On?' When his eyes narrowed, you wouldn't've thought he could see the camel, let alone the eye of the needle.

'On who you want to hurt more?'

'Wrong, Mr Woolf. Your premise is wrong. I don't learn anything when I find out Lewis is telling me lies. . .'

'OK, it's a fair cop, guv, you got me bang to rights. . . Except. . . You can't prove that I'm actually practising. . .'

'No. But your bank manager thinks you are.'

'Ah.'

DS Dowell – I had just remembered his name – had been working overtime. I'd change banks if I could find another one to take over the debt.

'He says. . . Of course, he could be a liar too. . . We could always pit your word against his. . . He says he loaned you money on an assurance that you were going back to work as a solicitor. . . And, indeed. . .' He reached into his Marks & Sparks jacket and pulled out his notebook:

'That you told him you had the promise of work from a property company . . . Called. . . Drakus Barkell? Is that right?'

"So?"

'So obtaining a bank loan by deception is obtaining a pecuniary advantage by deception is an offence under the Theft Act as. . . I think. . . You. . . Must. . . Know . . .' After a long, melodramatic pause, he added:

'Sir.'

It makes me very unhappy when people call me sir. I know it can't be genuine respect, so it's gotta be a put-down.

'You. . . Uh. . . You've discussed. . . This. . . Er. . . Aspect with my bank manager, have you?'

'Certainly not, Mr Woolf.' He looked shocked as he flatly contradicted what he'd told me ten seconds before:

'Discussing a man's private financial affairs with his bank. Whatever next? Is nothing sacred, etcetera, etcetera. . . No. I merely made some discreet enquiries. He happened to pop out for a moment, while I was in his office. Left the file on his desk, you know. . . Careless. . .'

'Christ, he's got all that written down?'

Dowell nodded dourly:

'Contemporaneous note, I shouldn't wonder. . .'

Contemporaneous notes were admissible evidence in court. The odds in favour of twelve good men and true believing a word I said were lengthening as quick as we were getting through the S'Comfort.

'There is. . .no such company as Drakus Barkell, is there, sir?'

I grinned:

'Name came from an old legal magazine. But. . . You haven't come here to arrest me, have you. . .'

It might've been a question, but I was pretty sure of my ground. No detective buys a bottle of a guy's favourite hooch, breaks into his house and waits half the evening for him to arrive home just to bust him for a little bit of pecuniary advantage.

'No, Mr Woolf. . . Or may I call you Dave? No, Dave, I haven't. . . Nor've I come to put the bite on you.'

He was way ahead of me. I hadn't had time to think it.

'So?'

'So I've come to have a drink with you. . . That's all. OK?'

'Lewis. You want something on Lewis? I'd better tell you I don't know him that well. . .'

'Wrong again, Dave. I can have Lewis any time I want. I don't want. He's. . . He's useful where he is. . .'

He was, of course, a much bigger cake to take a slice out of than me.

My confidence had returned. He could've had me, but didn't want to. He didn't want money. That meant he wanted something else.

'You enjoying this?' Tapdancing.

He tossed his little head lightly, rhythmically, from side to side:

'I don't mind. You?'

I laughed:

'I ain't ate. I'm going to scramble some eggs, toast. Got a bit of bacon, too. You want?'

'Yup. Go down nicely on top of this.'

He followed me into the kitchen. Carrying this with him.

While I cooked, we talked about the usual things: the three Ws – weather, women, and wallies we knew in common.

We ate in silence.

Then. We got down to business.

'Art Farquharson. I understand you knew him?'

Dear Lewis. Such a nice, trustworthy chap.

'Wrong again, Davy. . .'

'I don't mind Dave. . . But Davy? Do you have to?' My father called me Davy. With his money he could call me anything he chose.

He chuckled:

'My name's Tim. The last person called me Timmy needed plastic surgery.'

'Well, Tim, give. . . *Genug mit der guessing.* . .'

'You've been hanging around Disraeli Chambers. . .'

'Ah. I don't suppose you'd believe I was briefing them on a case? No. I didn't think so.'

'Question. Why. Question. What do you know. Question. Where are you going.'

'Answer. Privileged. Answer. There's a lot of second-hand wigs for sale. Answer. If I knew, I probably wouldn't be here.'

'Let's talk wigs. Wishart was first. Then Creemer. Then Nicholas. Then Farquharson. Four deaths. Right?'

'Right. What else do you know?'

He sighed:

'Not enough. They don't seem to trust me. As far as they're concerned, it's a lot of coincidence. They spend so long in court telling juries we're stupid or liars, they've begun to believe it. What do you think?'

'I think maybe you ain't necessarily stupid. . .' I passed on the other.

'A guy in the station. . . Few years back. . . In his locker. . . Had this cartoon pinned up. . . Showed two hippy types returning home and finding they'd be burgled. . . The guy's saying: "We've been robbed – call the pigs. . ." Geddit?'

'Well? They're not. . .'

'No. That makes me suspicious. Doesn't it?'

'What do you say?'

'I used to say: Wishart was a well-roasted accident. The coon cooled Creemer. Nicholas? Well, all right, let's say I was getting suspicious. But. . . He wasn't too drunk to ride his bike. And whoever fucked the faggot's got a funny sense of humour.'

He'd told me nothing.

'Why did the police go along with a coroner's cover-up?'

'To help me. Even if you've got an accident verdict, you can still prosecute for murder. It has no real effect. Except to make whoever it is feel a little safer. . .'

'Equals careless?'

'That's the usual scenario. Who're you working for?'

'Mrs Nicholas. . .' What the hell. He'd find out sooner or later.

'What do you figure?'

'I figure on giving up the case. It's way out of my league. One thought . . . A sometime member of the group? There's a few who've left. . . In a not-so-happy atmosphere. . .'

He shrugged:

'Would any barrister have the bottle?'

'You're the copper. . . You tell me.'

He poured us both another drink:

'What else do you think?'

'What do you want from me?'

'You've got contacts. . . You're one of them. . . They'll talk to you . . .'

For the first time it occurred to me. He was a little jealous. I was a solicitor. A professional. He was, after all, just a pig.

'Which means?'

'Which means we work in two ways. I stay outside. . .'

'And I work inside?'

'Clever boy. . .'

I thought this over for a long time. Say, ten seconds?

Tell me, officer, Detective Sergeant, Timothy dearest, or whatever you want me to call you. What happens if I decline to assist you in your enquiries?

Well, sir, you remember that business about the bank manager. . .

'I said,' he reminded me:

68

'What else do you think?'

I couldn't see the harm in telling him:

'A grudge against those chambers. . . Yeah?'

'Probably. Why?'

I gave him the last Wednesday. He hadn't known about the regular chambers' meetings, although he had put the dates together.

'Let's narrow the field down a bit. . .'

'Give. . .'

'Take the four who are dead. Wishart and Creemer were in at the start, right?'

'Right.'

'But Nicholas came later, and so did Farquharson.'

'Right.'

That gave us a date to start from. Whatever we were talking about was no earlier than when Farquharson – last of the four to join the group – had done so. As an end-date, we could take when it started, when Wishart died, the first to go. Six years: 1976–1982.

'It's a lot of time. . .' My lack of enthusiasm was ill-concealed.

He shared out the remains of the bottle:

'You scared of hard work, Dave?'

I shook my head:

'Not hard work. . .' I paused, then asked:

'You been following me?'

'Me?'

'Your people. . .'

'It's a funny thing, Dave. If everyone who was being watched by the police really was being, and everyone who thought their 'phones were tapped was right, and everyone who swears the police open their post. . . You know? Nothing else'd ever get done.'

'I didn't ask about anyone else. . .'

'Sorry, counsellor. No. Are you sure you're being followed? It's easy enough to think. . . If, maybe,' he grinned:

'You're a little nervy. . .' Spelled scared.

I threw what was left of my drink into the back of my throat:

'Yes. I'm sure I'm being followed. And. By someone who knows my movements before I get there. . .'

It was a fair guess. Gimbo might've followed my taxi from home to Harrods. But I hadn't found one till I was already on the Old Brompton Road. Where would he have been parked? Could he have gone back for his car and caught up with my cab? He hadn't even tried that game with Mrs Nicholas.

For the first time, I had a feeling I'd caught Dowell off balance. His face was normally pale enough for the difference to be hardly discernible. But I could've sworn he blanched.

All he said though was:

'I'm not having you followed. I've not tapped your telephone. All right?'

I shrugged:

'Then who is?'

He didn't even bother to deny knowing. Picked up his glass, drained it, got up and walked out of the flat. He hadn't given me a number to reach him. He'd be in touch with me.

It was late. I went to bed so's the hangover didn't start before I had a chance to sleep some of it off.

I've told all I knew by the time I saw Anne. Nothing else happened. I learned no more. Before I met her, I'd made up my mind to tell her what I was really up to. What I didn't expect was her reaction:

'Who's paying you?'

'How many of you people have got to die before you do something about it?'

A lot of silence. A little meaningless chatter. Then she said, softly, going straight back to the question and counter-question that counted:

'Alex already is.'

Chapter Five

At the end of the week after I saw Anne Godwin, Russel Orbach was in Oslo.

I know, because I was there too.

When I saw him, he was with an elderly lady.

I wasn't. I was with a young one. Marguie Bradkinson.

I wasn't too sure what I was doing there. Until I saw him. Then, I began to have an idea.

I began to feel not so very different from how I felt immediately after Anne Godwin told me:

'Alex already is.'

Stupid.

I'd been set up.

And, it felt like: not for the first time.

'Alex already is.'

I repeated the words after her like an incantation. Like she was teaching me the language. I had this image of a massive concert hall, filled with people, all chanting:

'Stupid. Stupid. Stupid.'

The whole world was ahead of me. Only I had taken so much time to work it out I thought it was the biggest mystery since Peter asked Paul:

'Who shopped the boss?'

(If I'd been given the case, you'd still be wondering.)

I contemplated my shoes.

They were big, to fit big feet.

They could do a lot of walking.

Like. South of the river?

I put these suicidal prospects aside and comforted myself with the thought that if I'd realized sooner just what a secret it wasn't, I'd be down more than a thousand pounds.

'Tell.' The command spat at her from behind gritted teeth.

She'd been watching me think. It was that obvious. The wheels grinding.

She shrugged:

'What's to tell?'

She was evading the question.

The penny dropped. She hadn't sensed how stupid I felt. The penny climbed back into my pocket. The whole world wasn't ahead of the game. Only them. And me.

'Forgive me, sweetheart. . .'

I paused to give her time to tell me to lose the language.

She didn't.

Then I knew for sure she was on the defensive.

I lowered my voice, to about where the penny had rolled:

'There's someone out there,' I waved a hand expansively as if to take in the skies, till I remembered abashedly we were in the confined well of an enclosed market: 'who don't just want you dead, but is getting on with the job like he was being paid piece-rate? Diggit? You know about it. Right? Well, there's one tiny question, not, perhaps, the most important in the world, but just one wee curiosity that's niggling away in the back of my mind. Who?'

She shrugged again. Maybe it was some new kind of esoteric exercise: I-shrug. Like I-sometric.

I tried again:

'Let's start at the beginning. What do you know?'

'We know. . . We know someone's. . . Got it in for us. . .'

She had the grace to blush at how lame it sounded. Like some solicitor wasn't sending them work no more. Or a friend was badmouthing her behind her back.

Spreading foul rumours. Such as that she'd once had a scene with me.

The conversation didn't pick up. I squeezed out of her that: after Jack died someone spotted the dates; their suspicion turned to certainty the night Art Farquharson took a shit the wrong way round; and – they hadn't told the police.

'Why not?'

She bit her lower lip.

I-bite?

'Anne,' I said gently:

'I'm asking you why not. If you don't answer me, I'm going to ask you again, now, here, and real loud – how come you ain't told the police there's been four murders? You want me to repeat the question? How come you ain't told the police there's been four murders?'

The second time I raised my voice just a bit. Just enough to make the point. She didn't give me the chance to try-out for cheer-leader.

'People. . . People are afraid. . .'

'I should think they are. . .'

She shook her head:

'No. That's not what I mean. Yes. They're afraid that way too. But. . . They're afraid of what will happen if it gets out. . .' She was almost whispering by the time she finished.

I still didn't get it.

'You know. Can you imagine? If this gets into the papers! Even if it just gets around the profession! We'll never get another brief!'

I was about to tell her she ought to practise advocacy at the funny farm. Trying to get in. But there was something in it.

The law's a strange business. It's a small world. Very small. There's maybe thirty, forty thousand solicitors, but most of them are out of London or south of the river and don't count. And there's only three or four thousand barristers. Most of them in London, in chambers in the Inns of Court. If one of them farts in open

73

court the others have heard about it before the smell's been swallowed up in the smog.

It'd take no time for this to reach the ears of every solicitor, every barrister and every judge that matters. What'd happen then? Well. You might think. It'd earn them a lot of sympathy. It doesn't work like that. You see. Lawyers are human beings. They'll react normally. They'll figure: one, the chambers must've done something pretty bad to someone; two, we don't want to get caught up in any scandal; three, maybe whoever's doing it'll turn on anyone who's associated with them – like a solicitor who sends them work; four, who wants to waste time instructing someone who may be dead by the time the trial starts?

Of course it wouldn't be a hundred per cent. There'd be the ghouls. The nutters. The peepshow artists. The vicarious thrill merchants. They'd still bring them work. Just to be able to hang around. Just to get in on the act. You can imagine for yourself the sort of work they'd be doing, and the sort of creeps that'd be bringing it to them.

I could see their point of view. But:

'Does it really add up to enough not to report it to the police?'

'I don't think so. But. . . Well. . . The others. . .'

'Does everyone know?'

I meant: everyone in chambers.

She shook her head:

'No. There hasn't been a chambers' meeting since. . .'

For the first time, she laughed, though not what you'd call wholeheartedly:

'If everybody knew, I don't suppose there'd be another chambers' meeting ever again.'

I ignored the competition. Making jokes was my job.

'Who does know?'

'Alex.' Obviously. And obviously she'd name him first.

'Gerry Gilligan.' That figured.

'Harry. Mick.' Barron. One of Jack Nicholas' contemporaries and, as such, one of the longer-serving goons.

74

'Jane Daws. Do you know her?'

'I saw her in the pub.'

'Marguie Bradkinson?'

'Yup. Her too.'

Leaving aside the last couple of names, she'd listed all the weight in chambers. The older, more senior members. Those with influence. That is to say. Those who were left. It made a point:

'They're being taken off the top. . .'

'Yes. It seems that way.'

'Gilligan? He's with you. Thinks you ought to tell the police?' Gilligan wasn't senior, but it was clear to me that he wielded influence. As did Anne. They got in to the club through ability, not age.

'You can never tell what Gerry's really thinking. I think he agrees. We usually do.'

'Then the negs are Keenan, Harry and Barron, right?' I didn't bother with Daws or Bradkinson: we were concerned with the thinking members of chambers.

'Yes.'

'Are you going to take it to the full group?'

'It's difficult. If we do. . . People talk. . . You know how it is, Dave. Everyone tells someone else. Confidentially of course. We might as well report it or publish it as tell the whole group.'

'But I know now. . .'

'Yes,' she sighed: that was a problem.

'You haven't told me. . .'

Who was paying me.

'No. I haven't.' Meaning: I wasn't going to.

'What happens now?'

'About?'

'About everything. What do we do? What do I do?' About me knowing.

'What do you want to do?'

'Tell Alex. . .' Run to daddy.

'I want. . . I want a little more time, Anne. I want to think things through.' I shifted gear:

'What's your best guess?'

75

'Someone who's got a hell of a grudge against the group. . .'

I admired the understatement.

'I don't know,' she emphasized 'know' the way I had with Mrs Nick – a lawyer's trick. It stank of false humility. I, a lawyer, wish to make clear that I am not talking about what I know. Ergo. You cannot hold me responsible for having said it. But I am a lawyer. The fact that I am saying it at all is a very strong indication that there's something in it. Whether based on unrepeatable or unusable information, or merely an educated guess, isn't something you can ask. Because I'll only answer:

'I don't know. . .'

'But?'

'Maybe. . . A former member?'

That was what I'd thought, too; till Dowell had damned it with faint praise – not enough bottle. Because I knew I'd never have the courage to cream anyone, I'd accepted his answer with alacrity.

'Is that possible? Can you think of anyone?' In particular.

'No,' she said, after a split second's hesitation.

She asked:

'Are you going to the police?'

'Not for the time being.'

I didn't need to lie. The police, after all, were coming to me:

'I'm not instructed to. . .'

'Yeah. You always do what you're instructed. . .' I sometimes didn't used to.

She picked up her glass. It was empty. Held it up to me to ask: another bottle?

'Sure. . . Why not.'

She was not a happy lady.

We stayed until closing time. We walked up to the station together. Bought our two-zone tickets. At the foot of the stairs, where we took separate trains, from opposite platforms, she hesitated. Then asked:

'Wouldn't you. . . Couldn't I. . .'

I didn't help her out.

'Oh, hell, Dave, I don't want to go home, alone. . . I'm frightened.'

'It's OK,' I comforted her:

'It ain't a Wednesday. . .'

She scowled, and turned away without another word. It might've been what she said. It wasn't what she meant.

I got a rare full night's sleep before the 'phone started. In quick succession I had two calls I still wouldn't like to guess which I was more taken aback by.

The first was from the cutie, Marguerita Bradkinson. She was about to leave for court and wanted to catch me before she left home. Sorry she didn't have much of a chance to talk to me in the pub the other night. Very interested in what I was doing. Would I. By any chance. Be free that evening. To come to dinner. At her house.

The second was a blast from the past that caught me just as I was going back to sleep again:

'Dave?'

'Ug.'

'Dave, this is Sandy. . .'

Sandy? Sandra? Sandra Nicholl? My former partner? The woman who had personally, single-handedly, totally and utterly destroyed my career without hardly a helping hand from me? That Sandy?

'Come again?'

'C'mon, Dave. I still recognize your voice. . .'

'I don't know. . .'

'What don't you know?'

'Whatever it is you want. Where the files are? What barrister I instructed? Whether we won or lost?'

She laughed:

'I don't want to know anything, Dave. . .'

'Then give. What do you want?'

'You're not being, well, very friendly, dear. . .'

People don't realize how like spouses business partners are. They know everything about you. What clothes you've got. What you like to eat or drink. What makes you tick. How you'll react. What sort of mood you're in. Even why.

'As I recall, we weren't on very friendly terms when last we spoke. . . Dear. . .' I threw back to see how it bounced.

'No. Well, that's past. . .'

'Maybe for you. . .'

This's another of my great, unique wisdoms. When people put the boot into you, it's a one-off action. They forget they ever did it. But if you're on the receiving end, the sting settles in for a long stay. You gotta live with the consequences. Maybe forever.

I didn't bear Sandy any grudges. She was right in what she did. I wasn't doing the firm any good. More important than that, I wasn't doing the clients any good. Most important of all, I wasn't doing me any good either.

'How are you, Sandy?'

'OK. I guess. I'd like to see you. Are you free for lunch? I'll buy. . .'

Two meals in one day. I'd burst.

We met in High Street Kensington. A new restaurant. Posh. Expensive. I'd never been inside before.

She was there before me. She looked good. She was in a dark suit which meant she'd been to court. Her hair was permed which she didn't used to do. But she still didn't need any makeup. And hadn't put on a pound.

We'd never made it. There were times when I wanted to, and maybe when we came close. There were times when I suspected she wanted to, and perhaps not even just casual. In the days when I thought I was the next best thing to Paul Newman (actually, it was Kris Kristofferson), I used even to wonder whether setting up in practice together wasn't some form of sublimation – on her part of course.

She got up as I fumbled my way to her table. Came around it. Took my hands like we were long-lost buddies (which I guess we were – only we got lost a long time before the partnership broke up). Kissed me on the cheek.

She was making me nervous. We'd been together five minutes, plus five on the 'phone made ten. She hadn't torn my head off once yet.

While we chose, we chattered. I asked about her headaches: she'd always suffered from them, still did. I asked about the firm. It was just called 'Nicholl & Co.' We'd been going to call it 'Nicholl & Woolf,' but we could hear it coming – nickel and dime.

'It's doing well. . . There's a lot of work. . . There's five full-time solicitors, two articled clerks. . . Seven reception and secretarial. . .'

'That's big. . . How many partners?'

'Just me, Dave. . .' She looked me straight in the eye:

'My first partnership experience didn't work out too well. Made me a little chary. . .'

I grinned:

'You got out cheap. Look at you now. . .'

There was something about her I couldn't place until the waiter was taking our orders and I had a chance to sit back and watch. She was more confident than ever I'd known her. In the early days, when we'd started up together, just about everything she did cost her a high dose of nervous tension. She was wound up like a clock. Me? I was so laid back I didn't know if it was Wednesday or Friday on a Saturday.

'How's Bernie?' I asked after the waiter'd gone. Bernie had been her bloke for six years when I met her; a decade of loving service by the time we broke up. I couldn't stand him. He was an accountant and, by all. . . whoops, some said he was the best fiction writer in the world of figures.

'We split up,' she said defiantly:

'Soon after you. . . Left.'

'Ha. Left. Got my arse kicked!' I scowled, but gently, so's she'd know I meant her no malice.

'You look good, Dave. . . Better than I expected. . .'

'Meaning?'

'Meaning I heard you. . . Er. . . Had a bit of a rough time?'

I wanted to get the subject off me:

'And the other one?'

All the time she'd been with Bernie, she'd been having a scene on the side. On her side and on his too. I never knew who it was. Someone outside our world, she'd always said. Those times I didn't figure I was her one true love, I guessed this other guy was. The only thing I knew for sure was: it couldn't be Bernie. She had far too much good taste.

'That. . . That didn't work out either. I still see him, but. . . We don't. . . You know,' she laughed lightly:

'I thought we were supposed to be talking about what a rough time you've been having – not me.'

'Ain't no supposed to be. . .'

The waiter brought our starters. She was on weight-watcher's avocado. I was into herring and sour cream. She'd ordered Niersteiner, remembering, I guess, that was my favourite wine.

She held up her glass:

'It wasn't all bad, Dave. . .'

'Not quite. Cheerio.' I gulped at my drink, to hide the fact she'd managed to touch me.

'What prompted this, then?'

Turbot to follow. I'd forgotten how much I liked poached turbot. I was branching out. Losing my fear that the next meal would be the last meal and it had better be steak.

'I heard. . . I heard you'd been seen around. . . I've wanted. . . For a long time. . . I didn't know how to, what to say to you, you know? It wasn't an easy time for me either, Dave. Either before, or during it, or after. I've. . .' She grabbed my hand:

'I've missed you. Missed working with you, I mean.'

I could've been flattered. Instead. Suspicious. I didn't believe in coincidence. Remember?

'What is this, Sandy?'

She looked quite maudlin:

'We were very close, Dave. You were my best friend.'

'C'mon, c'mon. Give, give. . .'

She laughed again:

'You don't change, do you? Straight to the point.'

'The way I was brought up.'

She knew what I meant. Nicholl had been Nichstein when her grandfather landed in the East End.

'Where'd'you hear I was back?'

'Three places,' she said:

'Disraeli Chambers. Sue Cannon. And. A funny little detective sergeant from Scotland Yard.'

Like I said: a small world.

While we were still in the restaurant, she told me more about herself, the way she was living and working, and why she wanted to see me.

She was a single woman, mid-thirties, the sole proprietor of a successful firm, with five young lawyers working for her. Two of them had done their apprenticeship with her, and had only recently qualified. They were no problem. One of the others was temporary. But the two who had been with her a while were pressing to get into partnership, wanted a slice of the profits.

It wasn't, she said, meanness, though I got the feeling she'd hardened up since I left. Maybe to do with breaking up with Bernie. Or the other guy. No one else around. Had to look out for number one. It was, rather, that I'd been her only professional partner, and look at how we'd been. She was, she said, simply scared to take on two new people alone, both of them men, to find herself maybe the minority partner.

It rang true enough. No one falls out as viciously, as painfully or indeed legally as messily as lawyers. There's an old saying: the lawyer who acts for himself has a fool for a client. At the moment of breakup, that's what's happening, people are acting for themselves, and they do some pretty damned stupid things.

'Me? You want me back? After what we went through?'

She smiled wanly:

'Sucker for punishment, eh?'

'Sectionable, I would've said.'

She knew the expression: compulsory incarceration under the Mental Health Act.

It was the part of her story I trusted least. She couldn't really want me back. Could she?

She grabbed my hand again:

'You went crazy, Dave. You'd had enough. You were screwing more women, popping more pills, than a rockstar. You wanted out, dammit, Dave. It wasn't me that made you go. You. You did it. You forced me to do it. But don't tell me I wanted it to happen.'

'That wasn't how you acted outside court. . .' When she gave me five hundred and wrung out of me an absolute waiver of any further claims.

'Come on, Dave. The firm had more debts than assets. Goodwill and the last four months of a lease were all we were arguing about. Your outstanding bills amounted to zilch. Hell, you hadn't done anything for a year!'

'Yeah, yeah. That's old music. It doesn't sing why you should even begin to think of bringing me back. . .'

'Maybe I like you,' she said softly.

I snorted.

'Anyhow, what makes you think it'd be any different now? Huh?'

'I didn't say it would be. I'm only saying. . . What about giving it another try?'

'Jesus. You make it sound like we were married!'

'A firm's a sort of child, isn't it? Didn't you used to say that to me?'

'Yeah, sure, when I was trying to get you out of one of those damned moods of yours. You know? The "I just wanna be a little woman and bring up children" number. If you'd had kids with Bernie, they'd be long-firm frauding with the pocket money by now. . .'

After we'd eaten, we went for a walk. It was a warm, still slightly bright day. Only a bit overcast. Muggy. But in England you grab it when you can. We walked along to Kensington Palace Gardens, and through to Hyde Park.

We sat and watched the ducks. They were cute. There were a lot of people in rowing boats. They weren't so cute.

'Gimme the bottom line, kid,' I put on my best Bogey. (As in: Bogey goes to Wall Street.)

'Come back. See how it works out. Give it, say, a year, two years. . . Then we'll look at it. . .'

I finally sussed it out. I could be used to stall her insistent but would-be erstwhile employees. Dave may be coming back. After all. It was his firm too. He started it with me. We're going to give it a while, and work something out. We'll have to postpone any decisions on other new partners till that's been sorted. She couldn't play that sort of game with a stranger, an outsider: only with someone who had a claim prior to theirs.

I put my arm around her shoulders, and hugged her close to me:

'I just remembered why I liked working with you,' I whispered in her ear as if I was about to ask her to marry me:

'You're the most conniving, scheming, manipulative bitch I ever did meet. . .'

No offence was intended, and none was taken:

'That's the nicest thing you ever said,' she fluttered her eyelashes sarcastically.

I didn't take my arm away. Nor did she pull free. We looked each other in the eyes. Like they do in the movies for a couple of frames before cut to pink flesh and that delicious tension: will they/won't they (show her tits)? Something was stirring. It took me a while to recognize what it was.

She didn't resist. I'm not even that sure who it was finally took the plunge. Me or her. It was just happening.

'This is crazy,' I murmured after:

'I've known you ten years. . . We've had some of the worst times of my life together!'

She laughed:

'Such nice things you tell a girl.'

I shook my head violently. To clear it. Got up. Walked round behind the bench. She didn't move. After a while, I went and stood behind her, laid my hands on her shoulders. She reached up with her arms crossed over her body and placed her hands on top of mine.

That was when I thought I saw a familiar shape across the pond. Gimbo. I cleared my throat:

'I've got an appointment. . .'

All the same. I went round and sat beside her again.

She was frowning.

'What is it, Sandy?'

She shrugged:

'I don't know. I thought I had it all worked out. That it was just. . .business.' She laughed lightly.

'Look at me! Thirty six years old and acting like I've never been kissed before! That's all it was, wasn't it Dave? Just the wine and the sun and should auld acquaintance, eh?'

'I dunno, Sandy. These days, people always seem to be asking me questions I can't answer. It's worse than being back in practice. Nah. It didn't mean anything. Just like you didn't. . .' mean the offer to come back to work.

We both stood up at the same time. Looked at each other for a while. Then she said:

'Which way're you going?'

I gestured vaguely in the direction of Hyde Park Corner, the underground station.

'Fine. I'll go that way,' she turned up the Park, north towards Marble Arch.

I was too far away to tell which one of us Gimbo followed.

Three hours later, I was dining with Bradkinson.

I'd shown up late. Couldn't find the damned house. Hackney's a maze if you weren't born there. If you were, you probably never found your way out. I don't know what happened to Gimbo either: he was getting better at tailing me; or I was getting worse at spotting him.

I'd guessed it would just be the two of us. Dinner a deux. I hadn't guessed, though, she'd have such a fancy pad. Or, from the way she dressed, that she'd keep it so well. I was so obviously impressed she took me on the grand tour. It was a big house, plenty of plain wood, floors, doors, cupboards, window-frames. The wall-paper matched the blinds and in the kitchen, the crockery; in the bedroom, the sheets. Habitat or Liberty's. Off the main living room was a sun and plant room: glass, with creepers up and across the ceiling.

That was where she'd laid it out for us to eat. Formally informal. Studiedly casual. I stretched out on an old stuffed sofa like I'd lived there all my life. The room had that effect.

For a while, she made a half-hearted effort at talking about the politics of their chambers, my ostensible interest. We managed to keep the conversation on this tedious plateau until she'd cleared the main course away. Then she rolled a joint, to help us through dessert.

I ain't no literary genius and even if I was, I couldn't get next to a stoned conversation. Almost every time I've been good stoned (which is a lot less than all the times I've been stoned at all), I've wished I'd had a tape recording to play back later. The only time I ever did it, though, I couldn't listen past the first five minutes. Not that it didn't make sense. More that I couldn't understand why it had seemed so great at the time.

All I've got now is snatches of talk, a recollection of a rolling sea, floating fantasies, watching as if from another room as they turned into reality.

Her asking:

'How old are you?'

'How old d'you think?'

'Oh, really old. Like. More than thirty?'

I chuckled:

'Closer to forty. How old're you?'

There was a gap before she answered:

'Twenty-four. . .'

She was fourteen years younger than me. It seemed like a lifetime.

'What d'you want with me?'

She'd put out a bowl of nuts, a cheeseboard, and a

packet of After Eights. Our first physical contact was as our hands brushed, grabbing for more. We'd got the munchies.

'You aren't a very happy man, are you Dave?'

It reminded me of a scene in a movie. I played it over. Then I tried to describe it.

'Did you see The Big Chill?'

She hadn't even heard of it.

It didn't have music by people with names like Desmond Desmond, Thrilling Thumbs, Foul Foreskin or Carved Carcass.

'These sixties people. . .'

'Like you?'

'Sure.'

Another long break while I scanned the faces.

'One of their friends is dead. Suicide. His girl-friend. . . Your sort of age. . . I guess. . . And they ask her: "Was he happy?" She says: "I don't know. I haven't seen that many happy people. How do they act?"'

'No, then,' she answered for me.

'You didn't answer my question either. . .'

'I'm scared, that's all, I'm scared.'

Without either of us having admitted that was what I was really interested in, we both knew what she was talking about.

'Who told you?'

'I guessed. . .'

Maybe yes. Maybe no. Maybe it didn't really matter.

I went to the lavatory.

When I came back, she'd moved to the sofa.

It didn't call for a lot of imagination to stretch out beside her.

I stopped asking why.

At least. For a time.

I woke up again, in her bed, in the middle of the night. The digital radio clock was shining in my eyes. I couldn't find the dimmer.

I slipped out of the bed and padded to the door. Paused in the half-light thrown in through an un-curtained stairwell window. There was a full length mirror just inside the door. I've created world speed records zipping past mirrors. Tonight, I hesitated, glanced back, there was something different from the last time I looked.

I crouched back inside the sofa where it had all begun. I could've been cold if I'd chosen to take it that way. Instead, it was the edge that kept me awake. To think.

Things were changing all around me like a kaleidoscope on acid. Even I was changing. I was so used to thinking of myself as a drunken bum, a fat slob, a lump of camel turd a desparate dog wouldn't piss on, I hadn't noticed myself tightening up, losing weight, getting physically sharper the same way I now spent the major part of each day using my brain constructively, instead of trying to forget I had one.

Maybe, after all, it wasn't so weird Anne Godwin had been prepared to give it another whirl. Maybe what'd happened in Hyde Park that afternoon neither. Maybe this evening too. Maybe these things happened all at once or not at all: something to do with being turned in on oneself. Maybe it never rains but it pours.

Lot of maybes.

They didn't answer all the questions, though.

Like: why had Marguerita gone this far out of her way to pull me.

Like: why had Sandy been prepared to bait her line with an offer to return to work.

Like: why didn't Dowell reel me in, instead of turning me looser even than before.

Like: why was Disraeli Chambers every which way I looked.

Like: why did someone hate them enough to. . .

She didn't speak. Curled up opposite me in the chair she'd started out from. She'd put on a nightdress, to protect herself against the night, or against me.

I watched her. I didn't feel anything. Unless, perhaps, a little grateful because it'd been a long time since I'd managed to get it together with any woman. Otherwise, zilch.

If she'd said then:

'D'you want to go home?'

I would've said:

'Yup.'

If she'd said then:

'I'm sorry. It was a mistake.'

I would've said:

'Yup.'

Instead, she said:

'You ever been to Norway?'

'Where?'

'Norway,' she repeated.

Well, of course, Norway. Where else should we be talking about.

'Why?'

'I'm going there next week. . . Just for a week. . . I'm attending a conference, for a couple of days, and I thought I'd turn it into a holiday. . . You want to come?'

She said it casually, like to a movie or to the shops.

I guess my look asked wasn't this what was known as a little bit sudden. We hadn't even woken up next to each other yet, and there ain't no more acid test.

She shrugged.

She looked sort of defenceless and cute and sweet tucked into the chair.

'I was going on my own anyhow. . .'

'Where're you staying?'

'In Oslo. Some people Alex knows are involved with the conference. . .'

That at least would be true. Alex had friends everywhere.

I didn't even remember to ask what the conference was. Instead, just:

'How'd we get there, then?'

Chapter Six

'Where's Keenan?' I demanded as I stormed into the clerk's room.

They looked at me like I was mad.

I was. But not crazy: angry.

'Where's Keenan?' I repeated.

I wished I was an American detective. I'd've flashed 'em with eight inches of grey steel. Very hard.

One of them shook her head:

'He's away. . .'

That much didn't surprise me.

'Where?' I snarled.

They shook their heads in unison, like they'd been practising for vaudeville.

I wasn't going to get nothing out of them. I turned and slammed back out of the door, yelling over my shoulder:

'You'd sell your mothers.'

Downstairs, I walked through Gilligan, returning from court carrying his helmet in one hand, and a blue wig-and-gown bag in the other.

'Will you tell me?' I demanded, marginally but undiscernibly less aggressively.

'What?'

I repeated my question:

'Where's Keenan?'

To my extreme annoyance, he laughed:

'I told them it wouldn't work. . .'

I knew exactly what he meant. Norway. Bradkinson. Me.

Before I went, I'd made a date with Mrs Nicholas. Partly, it was out of a residual sense of honour: even if she could not listen, I ought at least to tell her what tune I was playing. Also, I needed her authority for this unexpected added expenditure.

We met in the usual place. I arrived early. The ponce in the pin-striped outfit gave me a knowing look. He figured he knew how I was making bread out of her dough. I scowled back, to let him know there were other things I could knead. Like his face.

'Thank you.' She sat in the chair I held out for her:

'Have there been any developments?' she was as quick off the mark as ever. This time, though, she explained, conspiratorially:

'The Reverend Nicholas has an appointment in town. I said I would come with him, to do some shopping. I have to meet him at four o'clock.' It didn't leave long.

As fast as I could, I brought her up to date: the conversation with Anne Godwin, and, somewhat more pertinently, that with DS Dowell.

'Did you tell him? I mean. . . That I. . .'

'I didn't have a lot of choice,' I answered, without elaborating. Like most civilians, she was under the impression that orders from the police superseded those from the holy ghost.

'Thank you. Yes. What happens now?'

'That's the other reason I wanted to see you. I want. . .'

I hesitated, unsure how to put this with delicacy:

'I want to follow a hunch. Someone. . . A member of the group. . . Has invited me to go away with her,' I dropped my voice for the last word:

'A lot of this. . . Detection. . . You have to follow your nose, follow the breaks. . . I saw her recently, the other day. . . Out of the blue, well, not completely, but anyhow, she asked me to go with her to Oslo for a week. I don't know. . .'

It was a lawyer's know.

'I don't know what it's got to do with everything that's happening. . . I don't know that it does. It could be, well, genuine, personal, but. . . Even if it simply strengthens my ties, gets me more information, I think it's the sort of fluke I can't afford to ignore. . .'

After a bit, rather sheepishly, I added:

'Or afford to pay for myself. . .'

It sounded lame. She could spot it too. I felt like I was under a microscope. She wasn't stupid: I was talking about a week away, with a woman, on her money.

I wasn't lying. I wasn't doing it for that. That might be how it was wrapped, and I ain't talking old newspaper. Inside was a sliver of truth. It all seemed too much, too coincidental, too happening not to take part in it.

'Do you know. . . what it will cost?'

'The fare'll be the best part of two hundred,' I admitted:

'I don't know, till after, how much of it will be your time. . .'

'Do I know her?'

'I don't think so. Marguerita Bradkinson?'

'Yes. She was at Jack's funeral. It's an unusual name. She's. . . a most attractive young woman, Mr Woolf.'

I swear she was about to call me by my first name. I'd also swear there was a smile between her lips.

'Would I be . . . doing something wrong, do you think?'

I knew exactly what she meant.

I laughed out loud:

'I'm no Lord Peter Wimsey. . .' He was the only investigator I could think of who was also supposed to be the perfect gentleman.

'Go.' She had made her decision.

'Thank you for telling me. You'd like another cheque, I expect. . .' She wrote it out on the spot and pushed it across the table to me.

I hesitated before picking it up. Covered it with my hand. Looked her in the face:

'Why? Why do you trust me?'

'Shouldn't I, Mr Woolf?'

I shrugged.

She got up to leave: 'But you can pay for tea today,' she smiled.

She got as far as the door before she turned and walked back to our table. She said quietly: 'When I came to see you. . . Only a little more than a month ago. . . I told you I didn't believe how they said Jack died. I was right. You found that out. It isn't easy. . . It isn't easy to go on with it now. . . I don't mean the money. . . But. . . We have to finish what we started, don't we?'

All the time she was talking, I was looking down at the table, not at her. I didn't look up when I answered:

'I wish you'd go away. I'm beginning to like you.'

'Is that really such a hardship, Mr Woolf?'

I raised my eyes, to meet hers: 'You think I'm doing this work, instead of law, because I like people, Mrs Nicholas? You must know. . . You must have worked out what sort of life I've been living. . . I don't exactly claim I was happy, but I slept nights. . .'

'And before, when you practised law?'

'I didn't. That's all. I didn't sleep, anyhow not naturally, not without a little help, and I don't mean what the doctor prescribed.'

'Because you cared?'

'Something like that I guess.'

After a bit, when she still didn't go away, I added:

'It doesn't matter. I'm not being paid to tell you what makes me tick.'

'Thank you.' She left.

We were flying from Gatwick. To save money. It was an early morning flight, and we stayed together the night before, at my flat.

I still didn't know what she was about. Between the first night, and the night before our departure, we'd spent one more evening together. She'd come to my place that time also. I'd even cleaned it up. She had a case in court the next day. She wouldn't stay over. We just talked about this projected trip. I'd got no more out of her about why she wanted me to tag along.

This time, we went to bed early, and fucked ourselves

92

to sleep, which in my case didn't take much. Just like the last time I slept beside her, I woke in the middle of the night, and got out of bed. I sat at the table where I'd talked with DS Dowell, smoking Camels, sipping S'Comfort.

Like that first night too, she was woken by my absence and came to join me.

'Tell me?'

'What?'

'Why are we going to Norway together?'

'I like you. Just that. Really. I've. . . Been alone for a while. It gets lonely in the house. I used to share it. . .'

I interrupted:

'How long've you had it? How'd you afford it?'

The part of London she lived in didn't cost peanuts. A few people had bought there before gentrification, when it had still been dirt cheap, but she wasn't old enough.

'Inheritance. I've been there about five years.'

'Go on.'

'I stopped sharing it about two years ago. Before that, there was me, the bloke I was with, another guy and a girl. . . Not together. . . It was all such a big effort. I had to spend half my time making up for the fact I was the owner, it was my house. . . Compensating, you know. . . The other half of the time was rows. I can't remember much good about when I shared it . . .'

'But it does get lonely?'

'Yes. I don't find. . . Relationships. . . Easy. . .'

'That's supposed to make you special?'

It sounded crueller than I think I meant.

'Sure. I know. But. . . I'm me.'

I'm the only one I know about.

'And?'

'And you seemed lonely too. . . Oh, that wasn't all of it. The chambers' thing. Of course. Gerry told me. About you. I'd guessed you were lying. I didn't want to go away alone. I wanted. . . It's difficult to explain. You're connected, but not connected, if you see what I mean?'

It made sense. I was part of it, because I knew about it. But I wasn't involved. I wasn't one of the group. I wasn't subject to it. I wasn't vulnerable. Like her.

'Now you tell me. . .'

'Why I agreed to go?'

She nodded.

I poured us both a shot. Drank mine. Needed time. Not to work out why. But what to tell.

'Mixed reasons. I've been in a lot of weird places, the last few years. I mean, in my head mostly. These last weeks, months, I've been coming out. That's a. . . Well, all right, lonely fits. Where I've been has been just me. Now I'm finding my way back in. I mean. . .'

I laughed:

'I didn't even know that was what I was doing, to begin with, and I still don't know if it's what I want. . . But. . . It is what I'm doing. So, I guess, I'm fumbling for how to be with people again. And. . . And you wanted to be with me. So, what the hell. . .'

'I'd do as well as anyone? To try it out again?'

She didn't seem to mind.

'Our. . . Intentions? They fitted. That's enough, isn't it?'

'You're being paid? To investigate? To go with me?'

Ruefully, I nodded my head:

'I wouldn't've had the money otherwise. . .'

'I would have paid,' she hissed, angry for the first time.

'Didn't like to ask,' I mumbled.

I got away with it. She touched my hand in apology.

Gatwick's the most unglamorous airport in the world. Especially at seven in the morning. When you go to Heathrow, you feel like you're really travelling. International. Cosmopolitan. Gatwick's a glorified bus-station by comparison. Package tours. Loud English, many of them drunk despite the hour, if they weren't football hooligans on their way to Hamburg they might just as well have been.

I'd never been in Norway before. Or any other part of Scandinavia. I always figured it as somewhere worth visiting. Fantasies about liberated blondes. It felt much more abroad than, say, France or Italy or even Greece; countries I'd been to so often since a child, on holidays, they were, like a woman you no longer have to try in order to get into bed with, territory already gained, familiar and, as such, susceptible to contempt.

The people we were to stay with met us at the airport. They drove us back to their apartment, slap in the centre of the city, in a ten-year old VW that looked like we might have to get out and push. They were full of questions about Keenan. I sat in the back, staring out, a bit dopey from want of sleep, gloomily wondering what the hell I was doing there.

The conference was the two days after we arrived. I was invited to attend, but declined. It was a disarmament conference. I'm not a believer. Not, I hasten to add, on grounds of defence policy. I look around me and all I see is scum. Different levels of scum, maybe, but scum just the same. My policy is: nuke 'em all, start over, maybe we'll make a better job of it next time around. We could hardly do worse.

It was the second day on my own that I saw Orbach. It was at the Munch Museum. Norway's artist, the way Grieg – I had learned since my arrival – was the nation's composer, and Ibsen their playwright. I wasn't there because I love art. I was there because it was raining, and cold, and I couldn't find anything else to do except drink myself into a stupor at prices so creative Sandy's ex might've thought them up as a way of increasing tax-deductibles.

It took me a while to place Orbach. If Disraeli Chambers hadn't been uppermost in my mind, I might even not have recognized him. I hadn't seen him for maybe five, six years. He'd aged, in that time, almost as much as I had. Put on weight, a lot of it. Was almost completely grey. He wore a Norwegian cardigan, an anorak over his arm, he was holding the elbow of a lady old enough to be his mother.

I crept up close. For the first couple of minutes, I thought I must be mistaken. They were speaking in

Norwegian. Don't ask me what they were saying. But just as I was about to quit, he stumbled on a sentence and broke into an unaccented English that left me in no doubt at all. His companion replied in English, though, as with many Norwegians I'd heard in these last two days, with very little trace of direct accent at all. Just a slightly musical intonation.

I stayed behind them throughout the exhibition. The rain had stopped and I yearned for the uncluttered, uncultured outdoors. They were doing every last painting, every etching, every last lithograph. They strolled out, and wandered back towards the town centre. I felt less self-conscious about following them than I might have done in London, where I'd be wondering what everyone else on the street was thinking. Even if I could've read the minds of these people, it would've been in foreign.

At Oslo's Central Station, they didn't go directly to buy a ticket. Glanced at their watches. Hovered by the newsagent. They were waiting for someone. He ran up, obviously late, and kissed the woman. I'd put money on he was her son. He touched Orbach's shoulder: old friends.

I was right behind in the line and still didn't hear where they bought tickets to. I stepped up to the window and mumbled:

'The same. . .'

'Hva?'

'The same. . .' I could afford to speak a little louder now they were out of earshot.

The gamble on his English paid off:

'You want the same place?'

'Sure. . .'

'Four kroner. . .' Not much. Therefore, not far.

'What platform?'

'Number five. . .'

As I hurried to platform five, I glanced at the ticket. Damn. It didn't tell me where I was going. Just where I'd come from. I had to sit in their compartment, make sure I saw them dismount. I'd've rather put some distance. If he paid me any attention, he knew me well enough to remember. The same way Disraeli Chambers was on my mind, maybe I was on his.

It was a small, local, commuter train. We weren't on it for ten minutes. They got off at a place called Ljan. They walked slowly, idly, happily, up the road, away from the station, down another road, without a pavement: Ljabruvn is what it said. I had learned 'vn' was an abbreviation. Therefore, Ljabruveien.

I hovered outside, a way down the street, freezing cold. What the hell was I supposed to do now? It was well past the time I ought to have been back at the flat where we were staying. We were going to a post-conference party.

Orbach came out of the house. He wasn't wearing his anorak or a coat; just the cardigan. He walked straight at me. As he approached, I kneeled down, as if to retie my shoelaces. I was wearing boots.

'Would you like to come in, Dave? It's cold out here. . .'

Ugh.

Er, well, hello, fancy meeting you here, in an Oslo suburb of all places, what a coincidence, haven't seen you for years, how're you keeping, sorry I have to rush, let's stay in touch, shall we?

I followed him into the house. He introduced me to his companions, explaining:

'They're very old friends of mine. Of course, in a way, so is Dave. . .'

'Would you like some tea, Mr Woolf?'

'A drink, I should think,' Orbach suggested:

'To warm you up.'

He was the one needed warming up. I never met so much sang froid in one place before.

He nodded at them as if to say: I'm all right, you can leave me with him.

'Perhaps we shall see you again. . .' The mother said as they left.

I had a feeling: not very likely.

'You're right at home here?'

He smiled:

'Of course. They are my oldest friends. I visit them each year. I have known them. . . Oh, for close on twenty years. Since. . . Since I was over here.'

Then I remembered. Orbach had not followed the conventional path of, say, Jack Nicholas. (Remember Jack Nicholas? No? Well, it doesn't matter. He wasn't very memorable.) He'd left school young, went abroad, come back and gone to university three or four years later than normal. His time abroad had included time in Norway.

'Every year. You come here every year? At the same time?'

'As long as I can remember. Originally, the older son of the family was my friend. Christen. He's in Bergen now. That's on the west coast, a long way. So I don't see him these days. But *Mor* . . . She was, well, something of a mother to me, and I grew very fond of the family as a whole. So. I come back. Each year. And *Mor* and I visit the Munch Museum. You see, they change the works around. He left so many, they can't exhibit them all at one time. And we go to the opera. This is the opera season, you see,' he added, in explanation of the timing of his annual visit:

'And we walk in the hills behind Ljan. And I breathe fresh air. And walk clean streets. And perhaps we spend a couple of days in their mountain hut.'

He smiled, like a man describing his own vision of heaven. Perhaps more aptly, a soldier home from the front. He was at peace.

'Now. I've given you some answers. Perhaps you'd be so kind?'

'Well, I feel pretty stupid. . .'

'Please. That's not my intention. You followed us from the Museum. Why? What are you doing here?'

'I think. . . Well, I know, now at any rate. . . I was duped into coming here. To see you, I think.'

He nodded calmly, as if he knew all along:

'Perhaps. Also, I think, to get you away from Keenan? What do you think? That too?'

98

'I think. . . I think maybe what I think ain't that well-informed. . . Not as well-informed as you, anyway. . .'

'No. Well. I've had longer at it than you. I know them a little better.'

I remembered something else about Orbach. The reason everyone hated his guts, at Disraeli Chambers and elsewhere. Because he always did know. Everything. And wasn't ashamed to show it. I never figured it, myself, as showing-off, in itself, or for its own sake. More like: this is what I know, correct me, improve on it, add to it. A man in constant quest for knowledge, who did not suffer fools gladly, or at all.

'What do you know?'

'I know that you have been investigating the deaths of four members of the group. I know, today, now, just this minute, that they want you to think I'm responsible. I say they,' he laughed:

'I mean him, of course. Alex. None of the others could tell the time of day if he didn't show them what the numbers meant.'

'And?'

'And what?'

'And are you?'

He chuckled:

'I wish I had had the guts to kill them. I hate the bastards. Every one of them. Except, perhaps, Alex. We were very close once. I don't think you ever lose that sort of closeness. And, well, I understand him, understand the way he's behaved, towards me, he had his reasons and they weren't all bad. But the others? I wouldn't piss on them if their brains were on fire. . .'

'But you didn't?'

'No, Dave, I didn't kill them. . .'

The young man poked his head around the door and asked something in Norwegian to which Orbach replied:

'*Nei*,' which I just about worked out meant 'no'.

He explained to me:

'He wanted to know if you were going to eat with us.

They are a phenomenally polite people, the Norwegians. I love them. If I didn't have such a damned parochial job, I'd live here. Come, I'll walk you back to the station, put you on the train. . .'

On the road down, he pointed out the sights, identified trees and plants, paused for me to look at a particularly fine house. We passed a man on his way back from work, who called out to him in Norwegian. He replied, relaxed, at home. I don't know how much of what he told me was true, but he wasn't lying when he said he'd like to live there.

'We'll talk again. In London. Not here. This is not the place, for me.'

'Do you know where Keenan is?'

He shook his head:

'No. Find out. Come and see me when you can tell me.'

Marguie was waiting for me at the flat. The others had gone to a party, leaving her directions how to find it. I went into our bedroom and started to pack.

'What are you doing?'

'What does it look like?'

'Why?' If I hadn't know better, I could've sworn she was genuinely hurt.

'I saw him. I've done what I was brought here for. . .'

'What? What are you talking about?' She took one last crack at conning me.

'How was it, Marguie? How was I supposed to see him? With you? Were you to take me out to Ljan, for a nature ramble no doubt, spot him by accident, leave me no chance to talk to him, something like that?'

She blushed. But. Said nothing.

'Do you people really think I'm so stupid?' If they did, they had cause.

'So what if I saw Orbach here? What was it supposed to mean? Tell me. I'd really like to know.'

'I don't know. I don't know so much. Geir,' the man whose apartment we were staying in:

'Geir knows him. They used to be friends. Through Alex. When Alex and Orbach fell out, Geir took Alex' side. It was Alex' idea. If you saw Orbach, Geir talked to you about him, you'd think, well, it would all come from you.'

'Where is Alex?'

'I don't know. That's the truth. It was all his idea.' She shrugged, she didn't need to spell it out.

At the door, she took my arm:

'I wish you wouldn't. Couldn't you stay anyway? I do like you, Dave, honestly, it wasn't all. . .'

I snorted.

'You don't even know if there'll be a plane tonight. . .'

'I'd rather sleep on an airport bench. You know? You understand what I mean?'

I was glad I said that. It made it better. When that was how I had to sleep. It gave it a sense of purpose.

I couldn't get on a flight until late the next day. There were only two to Gatwick, and the first one was full. I was ready to flake by the time I got back to the flat. I sank into the bath, grateful I'd forgotten to turn the boiler off. Though it was only mid-evening, I was planning on straight to bed.

I should've known better.

'You didn't send me a card,' was his opening accusation.

'I didn't know you cared,' I mumbled.

I was already half asleep at the time. If the bell hadn't woken me, I'd've been all the way.

'I thought,' he picked up the empty bottle of S'Comfort I'd bought in the duty-free at Oslo and been drinking from all day while I waited, on the 'plane, on the train, and finished in the bath:

'We might go for a little drink. . .'

I knew exactly where he meant. I also knew he would brook no argument:

'Who's paying?'

Drinks at Lewis' were as costly as Oslo.

'He is.'

'In that case. . . Would it trespass unduly upon your tolerance if I took a little time to attire myself?'

'You what?'

'I wanna get dressed. . .'

He muttered beneath his breath. Something that rhymned with hit.

It was, after all, the only thing I had on him. Professional superiority. I was, by profession, a lawyer. Ergo. A gentleman and a scholar (pace the odd marguie-doll that managed to scrape through). On the other hand. He was professionally a sub-moronic get. Though I did not doubt some native, perhaps even nurtured, nous, he was duty bound to by-pass it as often as occasion allowed.

Lewis was not amused at our double-act. It would seem that the good sergeant had omitted to inform him of the acquaintance we had fostered since first introduced.

'Tim. . . Dave. . .'

'Lewis. . .' I said.

'S'Comfort. . .' said Dowell.

'S'coming,' he flicked his fingers at the passé rabbit who'd served me the last time I was there.

'No thanks, Lewis,' Dowell calmly disinvited him.

Lewis shrugged his shoulders:

'Suit yourselves,' I would've sworn he swallowed a 'darlings' as he turned away.

'It's leave the bottle, isn't it?' She grinned at me.

'You got it,' I told her sloping tits.

'Fancy her?' asked Dowell.

I shrugged:

'She's about my mark. . .'

He knew exactly what I meant:

'No more lady lawyers. . . For a while?'

'Something like that.'

One of the reasons I tried to keep as much distance between myself and Dowell was an unfortunate characteristic that cropped up whenever I was obliged to keep him company. I had a tendency – terrifying enough in theory, regardless of the reality – to tell the truth.

'Holiday. Bradkinson. Marguerita.' He prompted.

'Ah. Pity about that. But.'

'Tell time. . .'

'Not much to. Met a very nice gentleman. Lawyer. Orbach. Name ring a bell?'

'And?'

'And. Keenan set Bradkinson up.'

'Why?'

'I figured, so's I'd be staying with a charmer called Geir I couldn't pronounce his last name, who was once a friend of Orbach's and still a friend of Keenan's and he'd fill my head with a lot of nasty tales about Orbach and lo and behold Bradkinson'd make sure I just happened to spot him lurking behind a clump of pine and I'd put two and two together and make four.'

Dead bodies.

'And?'

'And, Orbach figures, so's Keenan can play naughty games behind my back. So? What do you know?'

He frowned:

'Not enough. Not enough by half.'

'But you know things you're not telling me.'

'Maybe. Maybe there's others know things they aren't telling me either.'

'How'd'you manage to meet up with Sandra Nicholl?'

He sighed:

'Good looking lady.'

'Look, sunshine, you leave your fantasies out of mine.'

'They ain't exactly alike,' he said. He didn't mean our fantasies either. Nicholl. And Bradkinson.

'Tell you what. . . You met Lady H?' Keenan's wife.

He shook his head.

'Well. I have. You can have her. All to yourself. OK?'

'Not from what I've heard,' he muttered. He did not mean he could not have her; just not to himself.

It was the first concession he ever made to me.

'What now?' I asked.

'Another drink?' He poured.

Lewis passed by. Dowell grabbed his sleeve. It reassured me to see him so friendly with others.

'Come and join us. . .'

Lewis arched his eyebrows:

'Bored with one another already, dears?'

He'd had a few in between.

'And I thought I'd made the match of the moment. . .'

'Ere, guv, alliteration's my lark, innit?

The girl brought him a drink.

'What in the name of god is that?' Dowell asked.

'It's called a White Russian. Vodka. Kahlua. Cream.'

Dowell and I exchanged a glance, held our unadulterated glasses up to one another: bonski, down the hatch.

'Your fancy fairy,' Dowell began:

'Didn't dance. . .'

Everyone was elbowing in. Unfair.

'I told you all he knew,' Lewis answered:

'What made you think you'd get more out of him anyway?'

'You can't give someone ten years. . .'

'You can't take ten years away from them. . .'

I thought: charming, charming couple.

'Would anyone care to fill me in?' I began. Quickly, I remembered Lewis was present:

'Let me put that another way. Would anyone care to brief me on this?'

'You ain't got a practising certificate, remember?'

'Ugh.'

Lewis was confused. He knew less about practising certificates than I did.

Dowell relented:

'The little faggot who saw the car drive off. . . Had a little chat with . . .'

'Ah. What's he got that I haven't?' I asked Lewis. Pained. I'd wanted the same favour.

Lewis said:

'You really need telling, you already got the answer. . .'

'I want it straight, Lewis. . .' Dowell began.

I couldn't help myself:

'Hardly the right person to ask, I would've said. . .'
Dowell scowled.

'Was it a fag did it or not?'

'Nope. That's my first and my last.'

To make the point, he got up and left the table. Leaving his White Russian behind.

'You knew that,' I remarked after he was out of earshot.

'Sure,' Dowell admitted.

'So? Why'd you ask?'

'I just wanted to make him tell me.'

'You're a cynical bastard, Dowell. You know that?'

'Yes. I do. It's part of the job. You ever think about it? My job. All I ever deal with is scum. Murderers. Rapists. Heavy villains who wouldn't hesitate to blow someone's head off for half a thou. That's now. Before. When I was a wee baby suckling, as you'd no doubt call me, I spent my days and nights chasing after bag-snatchers, baby-snatchers, cop-a-feel and run merchants, people who'd break into your home and crap on the carpet. . . Don't you people ever think why we get like this?'

'Nice speech,' I answered:

'I suppose you think it's a doddle defending them against bent coppers, biased judges, and bloody juries? Or. That it's all fun-and-games dealing with battered women, beggars, booted out workers or plain batty tenants? Don't give it me, Tim, I already got it.'

We sipped in silence. And something I could've sworn was kissing cousins with mutual respect.

'You didn't answer my question about Sandy Nicholl. . .'

'It's no sweat. To "bump into" a solicitor. At court. They're the easiest coincidences. OK?'

'I guess. But why? Why did you want to?'

He looked at me like it was obvious:

'Because of Keenan of course.'

I shook my head:

'You're going too fast for me.'

'You were her partner. You know.'

'It's late. I'm tired. I slept on an Oslo airport bench

last night. I've been slurping S'Comfort all day. Don't play games, Tim. Just, you know, tell me, OK?'

He shrugged:

'I thought you knew. She's been Keenan's piece on the side for years; if anyone knows what this is all about, she will. . .'

I looked across at the waitress. She was well into her forties. Her tits could be used to mop the bathroom floor with. The tights probably hid varicose veins. Those stretch-marks would look like an ordnance survey. Maybe she'd fancy me. For my body. Or even just for myself.

Chapter Seven

Gimbo was back.

'Who is he?' I asked Sandy, as we peeped out from opposite ends of her curtained bay.

'Police. . . We've seen him before. . .'

I snarled: 'we' meant her and Keenan.

I wanted to say: he ain't police. How was I to know? Tim Dowell could be playing me for a patsy the way everyone else was. It was fast becoming a national sport. In which crippled geriatric mental patients could excel.

I rang her the morning after my return. At the office. She sounded surprised:

'I thought you were abroad. . .'

'Well, uh, you know, maybe I couldn't wait to see you again. . .'

She got my point.

After a pause, she said:

'Do you want to come over this evening?'

She lived in Kentish Town. Where it was raining.

I kissed her on the cheek. Which she let me. Deliberately, I kissed her on the lips. She could taste how little I meant it and pulled away.

Behind her back, as she led the way into the living room, I grinned.

Finding I knew things I wasn't supposed to was some consolation for realizing I hadn't awoken from a three-year slumber the man most likely to make it in multiple marriage since Henry Eight. But not much.

'You want a drink?'

She hovered at the sideboard.

'Want? No. Need more like.'

I didn't really mind about Marguie. She was cute. And sweet. And young. God she was so young. But I'd always known. Even when I'd admitted to Mrs Nick she was paying for kicks she wouldn't read about in my final report. It had never been nothing but hors d'oeuvres.

Sandy was different. I already knew I liked her. I could get along with her. At least, when I wasn't obsessed by not getting along with anyone. Self included. Finding out I could also fancy her put her into a class I'd never believed existed. What I'm trying to say is: I minded.

'You wanted to talk. . .'

'Whose idea was it?'

'What?'

'Everything. . . Everything from day one you rang me up. . . None of it. . . was you. . . Was it?'

She smiled ruefully:

'Some of it, Dave. . . You're not going to believe me. . . But. . . Some of it. . .'

'No, you're wrong.'

I had a flash of insight.

'I do believe some of it was you. The bit about coming back to work. So's you could put off your other people. That smells like you.'

She winced.

'You wanna tell me. Or you want I should tell you?'

'I'll. . . I'll tell you.' It saved a small slice of dignity. Not enough. But where she was at, even a small slice counted for something.

'I've been seeing Alex for. . . Years. . . It was him. . . All the time we were working together. I wouldn't. . . I wouldn't've done. . . Anything. . . Anything that might've. . . Hurt you? Misled you? For anyone else.'

I was supposed to be grateful.

'Was it true? When you said that you weren't sleeping with him any more?'

'Yes. That was true.'

She was the one who was grateful. That I'd asked the question. She must've thought it indicated interest. All

I wanted was the truth. The whole truth. And nothing but.

Keenan had seen through my spiel about the book: between one and three minutes after we'd started talking. If that long.

Keenan had set Sandy up to jump on my tail:

'Why? What did he want?'

'I don't know. He was very vague. He said he'd seen you again. Suggested maybe I ought to find out what you were really up to. He knew. . . I'd told him before. . . I sometimes regretted, well, the way the firm had gone. . . He said maybe I ought to do something about it. . . See you. . .'

She laughed, nervously, lightly:

'So, you see, you're wrong. The idea we might work together again, that did really come from him, at least just at this moment. But, and this is the truth, Dave, there was no more to it than that. I only did it, well, because it prompted me to do something I'd wanted to do for a long time. I didn't, you know, promise to report back to him or anything like that. I wasn't spying. Maybe he wanted me to, but I hadn't agreed. OK?'

I got up to refill my glass. The price ticket was still on the cap. I smiled:

'This's from before?'

She nodded:

'How'd'you know?'

'Ain't nowhere you can buy S'Comfort for seven pounds nowadays!'

She bit her lower lip nervously:

'Make me another drink, Dave.'

G-and-T, like the good English lady she wasn't.

When I took it to her, she grabbed my wrist:

'He. . . He never suggested. . . What happened, in the park. . . That's the truth, Dave. . . I swear it. . .'

'That's supposed to be some big deal?'

'That's supposed to tell you. . . Oh, shit, I don't know. . .'

I pulled my hand away. But gently.

We sat opposite each other in silence for a while.

'I wish. . . I wish I had got in touch with you before. . .'

I shrugged:

'I don't suppose I'd've been interested anyhow. . .'

Neither of us had said which we were talking about: working together again; or.

'It's a funny old world, isn't it, Dave? You can know someone so well, and not at all. Or, different sides of them. But.'

She smiled wryly:

'It isn't news to me that I . . . liked you. . .'

That wasn't news to me either. The news was. That I liked her too.

'Do you want to eat here?'

I almost said yes. But. It was the wrong thing for her to say. Trying to take us in one direction reminded me of the other. The one I was there to follow.

'You still haven't said why. . .'

'I've known, for a long time, about the killings. . .'

'How long?'

She hesitated. For the last time. Goodbye and hello.

'Since Peter Wishart died.'

I absorbed the information slowly. It meant a great deal. Since the very beginning, Keenan at least had known it was some kind of vendetta against the group. It didn't necessarily follow that Anne Godwin had lied to me. It could also be that Keenan had kept it from her, perhaps from everyone else in the group, until they, in their customarily slothful manner, had finally managed to work out the obvious.

'And?'

'And what?'

'And what have you known?'

She wasn't enjoying the transfer of loyalty. Despite myself, I was glad it upset her to tell me the secrets she had secured during the affair with Alex. I wouldn't have liked to think of her as betraying anyone – even Keenan – easily.

'Shortly after Pete died, Alex saw someone. . . A

110

woman they'd known before... A German woman who used to live in London...'

'Who?'

'Her name was Helga. She'd been, you know, around...'

I did know what she meant. Around lawyers, probably around all professionals, a scene, a circle, grows up; comprised partly of professional supporters – assistants, secretaries, clerks, students, even clients – it also has its social purpose. It's a mutually satisfying arrangement. Those whose activities aren't sufficient in their own eyes to sustain an adequate sense of participation latch on to the lawyers; the lawyers surround themselves with people, dependants, to massage their egos, and reassure them of how important they are.

In left-wing legal circles, that scene takes in a much wider range of hangers-on. There are those in related fields – law centres, legal advisers, lobbyists, journalists, political activists, for example.

Because politics (unlike law) crosses frontiers, and it is of the essence of left-wing politics that it ought to be a world-wide struggle. Around left-wing lawyers has grown up a sort of forum, an international, socialist jet-set – again, part professional (only, now, the profession of politics) and part social. It wasn't difficult to imagine a German woman called Helga fitting in, or just hanging around.

'Back in... Well, the early days of Disraeli Chambers... 1974, 1975, 1976... You remember... Didn't we even go to a couple of meetings there? Some of them were heavily involved in Baader–Meinhof, and the things that were happening in Germany. Particularly Alex, Wishart, Creemer and Russel Orbach...'

'Yes. I do remember. Orbach wrote an article?'

'Yes... Helga was involved...'

I shrugged. I didn't remember any German women. I would have. For all my cultural bias against Germans, I had a weakness for lean and fit cropped blondes. Helga would have registered. Either because she was. Or, disappointed, because she wasn't.

Sandy continued her story as she made us another drink. After she set mine down beside me, she went and drew the curtains, to shut out the sound of the rain. She carried on talking, standing behind me, her hands on my shoulders, needing physical reassurance. Not because of what she was telling me. Because she was telling me at all.

'Helga went back to Germany.'

'Where?'

'I don't know. She met Alex on a visit, here, a few weeks after Pete died. Naturally, he brought it up. She told him she'd heard about it. And. . . That it wasn't an accident. . .'

'How did she know?'

'I only know what Alex told me, Dave. She told him Pete had had enemies. In Germany. At first, Alex said, he assumed she meant right-wing enemies, possibly the police, but not necessarily. It wasn't what she meant at all. She told him: on the left. . .'

'But why?'

I got up, accidentally knocking her hands off my shoulders, and paced about. I was excited, because I felt I was getting somewhere at last. But confused. I didn't begin to understand the whys and the wherefores.

'No. I've never fully understood it either. The story is. . .'

'Alex' story?'

'Yes, in effect. Some of the German underground. . . The people who came after Baader–Meinhof. . . Believe they were betrayed. . .'

'By Disraeli Chambers? How? That's ridiculous! How could a band of English barristers betray them? They weren't defending them! They couldn't have had privileged information! What then?'

She slumped down in the chair where I'd been sitting:

'It's no good asking me. . . I just don't know. . . You see. . . Alex. . . Well, you've met him. The English upper classes are different from you or me,' she parodied Scott Fitzgerald's famous line about the very rich:

'I had an affair with Alex for, oh, the best part of six years... On and off... He'd come and see me late at night... Or, he'd tell his wife he had a case out of town and pretend to go off the night before, and instead come here and get an early train... We never went out together... Or away... And... I don't want to say he was secretive about what he told me as well... That's not really what I mean... It wasn't that deliberate... But for all the time I knew him, he never completely opened up with me... As if, well, he never could, perhaps never would, with a woman... Even a lover... It wasn't on, do you see? It wasn't done to tell your woman everything...'

'I don't want to hear about it...' I meant: their affair.

I was thinking about the idea of a betrayal from Disraeli Chambers. It wasn't as implausible as I'd first reacted. One of the consequences of the social set surrounding socialist lawyers was an incidental channel of communication. It acted as an information catalyst. It is part of the status, the chic, within such groupings to be better informed than others, to be the possessor of secrets. That is a contradiction. Because people – someone – has to know how trusted you are, on the left, and the only way of proving it is by at least occasionally revealing what it is you know.

I was standing at the sideboard, doing what came most naturally within reach of a bottle. She got up and stood beside me, again placing her hand on my shoulder:

'Just let me say this, then.'

Her voice was choking. I glanced round. She had tears in her eyes. I turned away. I didn't need it.

'We haven't slept together for years... He's gone on coming to see me... Turning up late... Like he did the night he talked to me about you... A bit drunk... Wanting... Trying to... You know. I just want you to understand it's me that's said no...'

'So what, Sandy? So fucking what?'

'You're hurt, aren't you, Dave?'

'Who? Me? Forget it. I don't get close, and I don't get hurt.'

We were both more than a little pissed. Otherwise, she might have let it go then. Instead, she whispered:

'Are you sure?'

'What do you want from me, Sandy?'

She grinned:

'You know. . .'

I did know. What she wanted. Just then.

I glanced at my watch. It was nearly ten o'clock.

She followed the movement of my eyes.

'What's that for?'

Was I going somewhere else?

I shrugged:

'I wanted to know what time to put down that I stopped work. . .'

She laughed: 'Bastard. . .'

'Do you still know what you want?'

She nodded. She was shivering.

I would have left. Only. I was too.

After, I lay on the bed, my arms folded back above my head. She got up to go to the bathroom. Pee. Wash. I watched her come back towards me. I was aware of the differences from Marguie. Sandy's body was no way as firm; when I ran my hand across her sallow skin, it felt like crinkled cotton, not taut satin. When Sandy walked, her breasts, though as big as Marguie's, swung heavily from side to side, instead of wobbling precariously but lightly up high.

She was real. In bed, she knew what her body wanted, rather than merely surrendering it to my pleasure. I felt: where she is now, what her body has become, is an arrival. In comparison, Marguie was at the beginning of a journey. Where she ended up would be somewhere so different she would have become someone else. Maybe that someone else would be an improvement; maybe not. The point is: the end was uncertain.

It was woman versus girl.

She lay down beside me again. Rolled over, and

placed her breast on my chest, crossed her leg over to let it lie between mine. To both our astonishment, I began to respond. She lifted her head to look at me, laughing:

'You ain't so old. . .'

'It's in a state of shock. . . Like a chicken twitching after its head's been cut off. . .'

'God, you've got such a nice line in sweet-talk. . .'

'You've said that before. . .' In the park.

'I'm sorry. . .' About the circumstances in which we'd re-encountered one another.

'It doesn't matter. . .'

'It does. I wanted this to happen. Oh, years ago I used to want it. But, since we met the other day. . . And now I feel, well, nothing can come of it. . . Because you won't trust me.'

I didn't answer. If I'd said, sure, forget it, of course I trust you, I'd've been lying, and she'd've known it. On the other hand. I wanted to trust her. You could've knocked me over with a feather. I wanted this to be happening. I wanted something to come of it.

She did things then that were her way of telling me what she felt, what she wanted, what was possible, without using words. I can't explain what was happening as she did so. I wasn't overwhelmed by pleasure, lost in lust, riding waves of passion or anything like that. It was a far calmer, more rewarding, more peaceful sensation. While it was going on, it was washing away the years between. Not just the last few years since I'd left the firm. But years before while I'd looked in every place but the obvious, that which was closest to home, for substitutes which had never come close to satisfying.

It was midnight before she asked:

'Are you going to stay?'

Her voice said please do.

I wanted to.

I had a job to do. Something like this didn't figure in how I was going to finish it off.

I got dressed again. She just put on a dressing-gown.

That was when I glanced out of the side of the living-room window, to see how the weather was doing. I called her over:

'Who is he?'

She came over to look out.

'Police. We've seen him before.'

I snarled at the 'we'.

But. After all. I couldn't remain angry about Keenan and Sandy.

He was standing underneath a tree, about fifty feet down the road, beside a car that might or might not have been the one I'd seen him drive off in after our encounter at Harrods.

I thought about leaving out the back. It would have meant burglarizing my way through someone else's house. Sandy's garden was surrounded by other gardens and houses as far as the eye could see. There was no access to the open streets.

Well, hell, I thought, it was time to resume the relationship. He hadn't been around since before I'd left for Oslo with Marguie Bradkinson. I waltzed out from the house, as if oblivious to his presence.

Where Sandy lived wasn't the sort of street cabs crawled down in the middle of the night. She'd offered to drive me home, or to somewhere I'd catch one, or to call for one to collect me, but I'd refused. The air would clear what was left of the Southern Comfort, and the confusion.

I was halfway down the next street before I looked around. I couldn't hear a car following me, so I figured he must be on foot. To my surprise, he still wasn't in sight. I crossed over, before walking slowly back up to where the roads met, in case he was just a bit further behind me than I had expected.

It wasn't so much astonishment when I realised he wasn't following me at all – at least, tonight – as chagrin. He was still in the same place. Watching Sandy's house.

That meant one of two things.

Either he was watching Sandy. Or else he was waiting for someone else.

If it was the latter, I had a fair idea of who that would be – Keenan.

If it was Keenan he was waiting for, that also meant two things.

Either Sandy hadn't told me the truth about the current state of their relationship. Or else Gimbo was way out of date.

The reasons I didn't want to believe Sandy had been lying to me don't need spelling out. I had one line, which was fixed in my memory, and which helped me decide not only that Gimbo was waiting for Keenan, and that he was doing so because his information was archaic, but that also said Sandy was right when she identified him as police. Last night, Dowell had said to me:

'She's been Keenan's piece on the side for years. . .'

Gimbo and Dowell were sticking their snouts in the same trough.

It told me something else, too. That afternoon I'd been to Disraeli Chambers, to try and find out where Keenan was. They'd professed not to know. Downstairs, Gilligan had claimed he didn't know either. It looked like: nor did the police.

It took me half an hour to find a cab. I was about to tell him the story about West Chelsea when I changed my mind. I wasn't that far from where Gilligan lived.

The lights were on throughout the house. I glanced at my watch. Only one o'clock. That's a time when sophisticates are still trying to select sleeping partners for the night.

I knew the woman who answered the door, though I couldn't put a name on it. She didn't recognize me either.

'Gerry here?'

She held the door back and stepped aside to allow me to enter.

Banged at the nearest inside room:

'Gerry. Visitor.'

It took him a minute to open up. Kept his body in

the gap so's I couldn't see in. All he was wearing was trousers. I grinned:

'Sorry. . .'

'I'll be right out, OK? You want to wait in the kitchen?'

The lady of the house led me down. By now she knew she'd met me before. I remembered her. Journalist. Left wing journal. We resumed acquaintance.

'Ah,' she said when I'd identified myself:

'You're the one that's writing about them. . .'

'That's right,' Gerry entered door right:

'You want some coffee? Good night, Sue.'

She laughed:

'So subtle. Good night.'

'Not a confidante, huh?'

'Who is? Who do you trust?'

'Try me. . .' I mimicked the airplane commercials.

'Why?'

''Cos you rang me that night. . . 'Cos – according to what you said this afternoon – you didn't figure me for a fool. . . 'Cos I'm insane enough to give up a week away with your colleague's tender young flesh to get on with the job. . . Any of them reasons do?'

He shrugged:

'You'd go stir crazy hanging out with Marguie for a week. . . She only knows one thing and doesn't even do that well. . .'

'Maybe her training wasn't that great,' I said softly. I had no brief for Bradkinson, but the evening had made me mellow.

For a second he dithered between anger and amusement, and, undecided, acknowledged:

'Fair enough. . .'

'Did it surprise you I came back?'

'No.'

'Why not?'

'Nothing does any more. . .'

'What's your game, Gerry? What do you know? For certain?'

'Too little. Like everyone else. Just that it's going on.

And. That someone'd better bring it to a halt before we're looking for smaller chambers to work from.'

"'S' that why you rang me that night? 'Cos you think I can sort it?'

His brow furrowed:

'I don't know. Do you know the reason you do everything?'

'I guess not. . .'

He was pretty close to why I'd taken up doing nothing for a profession.

'I know it's a grudge thing, against the group, but you don't need an elementary pass in detection to work that out. I know Keenan thinks its political. And. . .'

'German?'

He was impressed:

'Yes.'

'And?'

'And what?'

'Do you believe him?'

'Yes and no.'

Lawyer's answer. Covered all the available options.

'What has Keenan told you?'

'That Peter Wishart – and others – were mixed up in things German. One of their gestures of political solidarity. That some people got killed. By police. Members of a German gang. There were one or two survivors. Or the group had comrades. Anyway, apparently someone out there believes the way things happened was Disraeli Chambers' fault. . .'

'How so?' I'd got a bit more out of him than I already knew. Sandy's word 'betrayal' had been coloured red. I don't mean political red. Blood red.

'A date. A time. A place. Don't you remember it? I do: I was still at University. The police hit a house, claimed to have killed eight terrorists. . . It was big news at the time. . .'

I had a vague recollection:

'1978? 1979?'

'1978. After Ulrike Meinhof was murdered in prison. Before the others were too.'

119

I wasn't about to quibble with 'murdered'. As I recalled, even the straight British Press never bought the deaths of Ulrike Meinhof and, later, Andreas Baader and the remaining gaoled members of their gang, as anything other than a final sentence passed and executed not by the courts, but by the German police and their associates.

'And? Was there anything in it? Did Wishart know anything? Could he have leaked?'

'I don't know. I'd say. . . It's possible he knew. . . I don't know about the other. . .'

He went back to the kettle:

'You want another coffee?'

'Sure. If you are. . . I sort of had the impression you were being waited for? Anyone I know?'

'No.' He glanced around:

'You want to check?'

I shook my head. I couldn't think it mattered.

'You said: yes and no. What did you mean?'

'I meant. . . I can't really explain. I get an uneasy feeling. . . That we're still not being told the whole truth. . .'

'By Keenan?'

'Yes.'

'Tell me where Orbach fits into this?'

I'd put my finger on it.

'That's what I meant. You have to remember, I wasn't around when the split with Orbach happened. He's very bad news in chambers. All the ones who were around at the time hate him. They won't talk about it. If you ask, you get a different story each time. As if they weren't even totally certain how it happened themselves. Just that. . . Well, it was bound to have been his fault. Everything was. Everything bad before he left and. . . This is where he connects: everything since. He's like the chambers bogey man, the devil incarnate, whatever goes wrong, some people believe he must be at the back of it.'

'Paranoia?'

'Maybe. But you know what we used to say. "Just

because I'm paranoid doesn't mean they don't hate me.'"

Nor did it. I remembered Orbach's venom in Oslo.

'Who is it. . .' I paused, to try and form the question before I asked it:

'Who is it in chambers believes Orbach's involved? I mean specifically, in this, not just because of what you said,' about the assumption of intervention.

'You want me to say Keenan, don't you?'

'I don't want anything, Gerry. Except to get to the bottom of this,' and get it behind me.

'All right. No, not Keenan. At least, he's never said so. You see, there's no hatred between Keenan and Orbach. There never was so far as I can tell. . .'

'I heard, Orbach and Lady Helen?'

'Sure, I heard that too. But, well, Keenan isn't like that. I doubt he'd care, and he certainly wouldn't let that turn into hatred. Keenan. . . Well,' he laughed, and said something not so dissimilar to a remark Sandy had made earlier:

'I don't think he feels deeply at all. About anything. I mean, the upper classes don't, do they?'

'If Keenan didn't believe Orbach was involved, why'd he send me to Oslo?'

'From his point of view, just to get you out the way. Also, with Orbach there, it fitted with what others would like to believe. . . Keenan's a master of expediency. . .'

'Do you know where he's gone?'

'No. I said. I wasn't lying. None of us know where. But I know why.'

'Ah.'

'He's gone to meet someone. . . I don't know a name . . . I don't know a place. . . but you might call them an intermediary. . . He's trying to get through. . . To bring it to an end. . .'

'Brave man,' I commented.

After a bit, I asked him:

'Why not the police? Or do you also subscribe to the proposition that the practice is worth any price?'

I did, however, now understand what Anne Godwin had meant, even if they weren't the words she had used.

It was not the reaction of the profession at large that she was worried about. Just their bit of it. Their particular clientele. Much worse than some vague possibility of scandal, apparently worse even than a rather novel tax on membership, was the prospect of being held up as traitors to the left. Their practices were those of quote unquote radical lawyers. From what I had already managed to gather, those practices didn't amount to much at the best of times; since Orbach had left, they were based on Keenan's reputation alone. If something like this came out, what little there was would disappear altogether.

'What do I know?'

'You could have told them. . . Before they had to work it out for themselves. . . You might have one more partner. . . Or maybe you didn't care that much for Art Farquharson?'

He didn't bat an eyelid at the accusation:

'You can investigate me as long as you like. I'm not a murderer. And I don't know any more than I've told you.'

'You don't think much of them do you, Gerry? Why are you still there?'

He shrugged:

'It's not as easy as all that. All my life. . . As long as I can remember. . . I was a socialist. . . And all I wanted to be was a barrister. . . Crazy ambition. . . I ought to say: crazier than you know. . . It wasn't exactly the sort of thing members of my family went in for. . . My dad was a tailor. . . And I don't mean John Collier. . .' He named a major men's clothing chain store.

'I went to Oxford. . . On a scholarship. . . Got a grant through the Council of Legal Education. . . All the time thinking: I wanted to get in to Disraeli Chambers. . . I was going to get in there. . . And: I did. . .'

'And?'

It wasn't all it was cracked up to be.

He shrugged:

'It's a joke, really. . . They're no worse than other left-wing lawyers. . . Especially at the Bar. . . Poncing around playing politics. . . Patronizing their clients. . . Sitting around in meetings. . . Endless bloody meetings. . . Discussing Ireland and Palestine and all points East. . . Going to the pub feeling smart. . . Clever. . . 'Cos they're different. . . For half of them it's an excuse for not bothering to try: they lose because the court's're against them – or the client – never because they didn't work hard enough, because they just blew it. . .'

'Are they wrong?' About the courts.

'No. That isn't the point. The thing is. . . About being a left-wing lawyer. . . It's all in the way you fight the case. . . Above all, it's in the way you lose. . . You've got to win on the facts and law and force them. . . The courts. . . To show their true colours. . . That's when you're winning politically. . .'

'What about the client?'

'If it's winnable, what I said gives them the best chance too. . . The best professional chance. . . No?'

'Maybe. What's it got to do with the price of eggshells?'

'The ones that got cracked?'

'Yup.'

'It's all mixed up together. It's an unreal world. Look at the left-wing lawyer. . . We've staked our claim to being special, different, because we're left-wing. . . We're the ones who both know the law, and poke two fingers at it. . . That's our point of pride. . . But, all the time, disregarding the rhetoric, in fact we are barristers, lawyers, just like all the others, and that's all we know how to do. So we're frightened to go too far, frightened to jeopardize that status, to lose it. But politically, that's the one thing we can't admit to. . . It would undermine our claim to being more political than lawyer. . . It's a latent force. . . And it's a fear. . .

'I think things get very confused. The lines are completely unclear. Not between what's legal and illegal. . . We know that, just about. . . But between

123

what lines a political lawyer, a left-wing lawyer, ought to respect. On the one hand, you're being driven to show you're not a servant of the law, politically that you're just using it; and on the other is that fear. . . So who or what is there to tell you what to do, when to stop, how far to go. . . Across the line. . . In either direction. . .'

'What are you saying?'

'Just. . . That all things are possible. . . Maybe Wishart did know things he ought'n't to. . . Maybe he, or someone, did leak. . .'

'Which doesn't explain how Keenan thinks he can bring it to a stop, or what Russel Orbach's got to do with it if anything, or why you don't believe Keenan's telling you the whole truth, or, for that matter, assuming it all hangs together the way it's been spelled out, what we're going to do about it. . .'

He smiled:

'Meaning you don't like speeches that don't give you answers?'

'Meaning I've had an awful lot of them recently. . .'

'Where do you go from here?'

'Apart from home?'

It was pushing three.

He nodded.

'Keenan, I guess, when he gets back. When will that be?'

'I'm not sure. But before the next chambers' meeting. . .'

'Ah, yes. I'd forgotten about that. . . Maybe it ain't so brave to go, provided he gets back by Wednesday. . .'

We had the same thought at the same moment:

'How does that fit in?'

It was the feature that had made me think, earlier on: chambers' member.

We also had the same answer:

'Russel Orbach?'

'It does seem. . . Every time I turn around. . . He's standing there. . . Watching over my shoulder. . .'

'You're catching chambers' paranoia, Dave. . .'

'Yup. And. Every time I see him. He's laughing.'

Chapter Eight

The night of the next chambers' meeting, I had two invitations. I was growing popular. It was a pleasant sensation.

The first invitation – in time – was the one I did not finally turn up to. It came from the man who sometimes qualified as 'the good', but more often as something slightly more selective, such as 'that bastard'. By whom I mean to refer, as you will doubtless have worked out for yourself, to Timothy Dowell.

'How would you like. . .'

I held my breath.

This was usually the point in the conversation when routes violently diverged.

Thus, the next phrase might well be:

'To spend a week in the slammer picking your schnozzle. . .'

Or else, it could be:

'To get pissed at Lewis'. . .'

Or, with a little stretch of the imagination:

'A reward for all the good work you've done so far. . . From the informant's fund. . .'

As it was:

'To go camping with me. . .'

I paused for reflection. There were several available explanations. He had found in me the son and/or best boyhood friend he'd longed for but never had. He was as fagotty as Farquharson and liked it best in the open air. The murderer was a member of the boy scouts. He had finally flipped.

'You wouldn't. . . Er. . . Like to elaborate on your intentions, would you?'

'There's a four syllable word in that sentence, Woolf. I've warned you. . .'

'Sorry. How about: whaddayamean?'

'I mean this. Tomorrow is what?'

OK. You got it.

'And?'

'And I'm proposing we take certain precautions. . .'

'Like?'

'Would you believe I'm going to camp out in Disraeli Court? Me, plus two of mine to each of them?'

'Nah. You need a contract on the Queen for that sort of manpower.'

'One on one?'

'I'd believe you if you said thirteen of you to fourteen of them and you need me to make the numbers. . .'

He snorted:

'You think I'd trust you to follow one of them? I wouldn't give you to the first dark corner.'

'You could give me one of the men. I don't lose them quite so fast. . .'

He grinned wickedly:

'You only said that before I did. . .'

'Tell me about it. . .'

'You know Disraeli Chambers. . .'

I did indeed. These days: better than I could recall the layout of my home.

Disraeli Chambers was in one of the buildings in a courtyard – Disraeli Court – in the Middle Temple. There were about ten buildings in Disraeli Court, each containing between two and five sets of barristers' chambers, one or two with solicitors' offices, and on the top floor of most of them lived the odd geriatric judge or senior barrister.

At one end of the courtyard was the back of a big hall, where barristers dined, and ceremonial occasions took place. The main door of the hall was, however, outside Disraeli Court. There were only two exits from the courtyard, and from the buildings within it.

Dowell proposed to site his men in the basements of the buildings. They would be able to see anyone who left any of them, and follow whichever exit they took. His allowance was somewhat lower than I had estimated – a mere eight souls plus himself (who had no soul) – but he banked, on experience, on them leaving in groups, and several of them passing what was left of the evening after their meeting ended getting plastered in the pub. Once his men had escorted safely home the loners who went off in other directions, they would be able to return to duty before closing time. It was a gamble, but calculated.

I neither accepted, nor refused. I asked:

'Is Gimbo one of your men?'

'Who he?'

I described the man whose fidelity to me had proven so fickle, and that was now transferred – albeit aesthetically understandably – to Sandy Nicholl.

Dowell wasn't dumb:

'You asked me before if I was having you followed? Same?'

'Sure.'

He shook his head. Not guilty. But, just as on the previous occasion, not without a shadow fleeing across his face.

This conversation took place on the Tuesday afternoon. In a café near New Scotland Yard which Dowell worked out of. It ended with my provisional acceptance of the invite.

That was before a telephone call the next afternoon. From Lady Helen Keenan.

'Yes,' I confirmed it was indeed I.

'You don't know me. . .'

That was her first mistake. I had met her. She had forgotten. I sometimes forget people myself. Anyone can. But to forget me?

I didn't remind her. After all. 'Twas in another county, and besides our host was dead.

'But my name's Helen Keenan. . .'

That was her second mistake. She was the Lady

Helen. And no one was supposed ever to forget it.

'I was wondering whether we could meet, this evening. . .'

'It's Wednesday. . .'

'Yes. Alex will be at the chambers' meeting. . .'

She was not concealing that she wanted to see me without him there.

'OK. Where?'

'Could you come to the house? The children. . .'

'All right. What time?'

'The earlier the better. Six-ish?'

That would give us plenty of time to talk. Before Keenan got back.

Tim Dowell was out:

'Could you tell him his friend Dave rang and I can't make our date tonight?' I lisped.

Lady H led me quickly into the living room. It was five past six and the bottle of red wine on the coffee table was getting low. By it lay a corkscrew, and the cork, which suggested it wasn't exactly a long time since it lost its virginity.

'Shall I get you a glass?'

'Fine. . .'

While she was out of the room, I took a quick look around. The furniture was a studiedly casual mix. Some of it was probably antique; the sofa was perspex and plastic; on the walls, there were revolutionary prints, and framed pictures of the ancestors – Keenan's and hers; the dining table was stainless steel, but the chairs tucked beneath it covered in velvet.

On the open bureau lay an airline ticket. I was just about to read it when I heard Lady H's heavy-breathed return. Instead, I swept it beneath my jacket, and thence into my wallet pocket. Too bad if it was unused: there was enough mess about the room to lose the Crown Jewels, let alone a thin folder of paper. If it couldn't be found, doubtless it could be re-issued.

'You wanted to see me.'

It was her job to open.

I sipped the wine carefully. Red wine doesn't agree with me. Bad red wine makes me violently ill. I placed it gingerly on the table. Just looking at it made my stomach churn.

Lady H was a startling woman. She attracted, without being attractive. Like a blazing fire attracts a child. She had a mess of auburn hair tumbling about her hawk-like head, perched on top of a body that resembled a dumpling more than an hour-glass or a pear. When she walked – as when she had re-entered the room – it was as if she was fighting the air-space to get through. She spoke much the same: ill-concealed, but possibly impersonal hostility; habitual aggression; defiance.

'You're investigating the chambers' murders,' she stated matter of factly.

These days it was about as much of a secret as the location of Buckingham Palace.

'OK.'

'I want to tell you about Russel Orbach,' she continued, ignoring me, and as if the connection was obvious.

I didn't say anything. After all. Words cost energy. Energy is to be conserved.

'Russel Orbach is a vicious, cruel man, who hates my husband, and who hates me.'

The last person who'd remarked on Orbach's hatred was Gilligan. He said Orbach hated chambers. He was correct. I know. Because that was what Orbach had told me. Orbach had also said: he didn't hate Keenan.

She waited.

I waited.

I gave in first:

'Why?'

'Orbach is a maniac. He's very clever. I'll grant him that. Brilliant if you like. But inhuman. He's conceited. He thinks he's the cleverest, and most important, man in the world. For years, he conned all of us: particularly Alex, and me. He made us believe in him politically, and professionally, and even personally. All his difficulties – and he's a difficult man, God knows – had to be forgiven, overlooked, he had to be helped through them. . . Personal problems, emotional, psychological, professional. . . It was everybody's else's duty to comfort and protect him. . . Especially ours. . .

'You must have met people like that. It's never easy to know if they really are worth helping, because they really are gifted people – the awkward genius! – or if they're simply egocentrics demanding attention for no greater end than itself. . . Or plain mad, bad or selfish. . .'

I wasn't very comfortable with this part of her statement. It was a little too close to home. I could recall, in my professionally successful days, more than one girlfriend making similar observations about me, usually in the middle of a terminal row.

'Sometimes, you never find out. Sometimes, you can only find out by looking back on what they've actually done with their lives, in their work. Most great men have been difficult. But, sometimes, they make a mistake, reveal their true personalities, show themselves for what they really are. . .'

'And Orbach? That was what he did?' Left to herself, she might continue to develop her thesis for longer than we had left. I wasn't convinced she didn't like the sound of her own voice as much as, by implication, she was saying Orbach did.

'Yes.'

'How?'

It was, at least in one sense, the sixty-four thousand dollar question. The answer was worth about two bits.

'He raped me. Here. In this house. In front of the children.'

I had to say something.

I thought quickly.

'Ah.'

It wasn't, perhaps, profound. But. It came closest to expressing just how shocked I was.

'Here? In front of the children?'

You read about this sort of thing. It does happen. It can happen when a child is tiny. Or if the rapist ties

130

the children up first. Or if he's got a gun or another weapon. Somehow: it would not focus with Orbach's face in the frame.

'Well, they were upstairs, in bed. . .'

Edit one.

'Didn't. . . Didn't you cry out? Didn't they hear?'

'It wasn't. . . Well. . . It wasn't a physically violent rape. . .'

Edit two.

I was beginning to enjoy this. Your starter for ten points: what is rape without physical violence, in front of the children who are in another room?

'A woman can be raped in ways other than with physical violence, you know Mr Woolf. There are other ways of overriding what the woman wants. Negating consent. Conning someone. Persuading them they want something, when they don't.'

I nodded. I'd heard. I'll go further. I even accept it. But Lady Helen? By Orbach? It simply wasn't credible. She was – on present performance and past recollection – one very tough lady, who knew her mind and didn't allow anyone – including Keenan himself – to tell her what was in it.

She filled in some local colour. Orbach had been involved in a long inquiry. Earning a lot of money. Attracting a lot of media coverage. He had been working hard. Drinking. Hyped up. Full of himself. Come around one evening. Keenan had been away for the weekend. She'd not wanted to let him in. He was already drunk. He'd insisted on coming in.

She'd gone on drinking with him to keep him company. He'd been angry with Keenan: some petty dispute over chambers' politics. He'd started attacking Keenan, abusing him, in front of the children. She'd sent them upstairs. Still he wouldn't go. In the end, she left him. Went up to see one of the kids. When she came back down, he was in their bedroom, in the bed, waiting for her.

'I felt sorry for him. He obviously couldn't cope with all the responsibility of the inquiry. He'd told me he could hardly get it up any more, because he was too tired from the strain. I didn't know what to do. It was a habit to want to help him, to let him have whatever he wanted, so I did. . .'

Her son had heard them. Stood outside the door. Called out. They'd stopped. He'd left.

'I couldn't explain. . . To John. . . My son. . . I couldn't explain to him how Orbach could have behaved like that. He couldn't understand. How could he understand? It was because of that, because of John, that I couldn't go on covering up for Orbach any more. . .'

She'd told Keenan. He had been reluctant to accept how it had happened. He didn't want to believe ill of his professionally blue-eyed boy. Orbach had been his pupil, then his favourite son. He had been his most successful trainee. He had become his closest ally in chambers, confidante, supporter, even, on occasion, someone whose lead he could himself follow.

She had gone to the group. She had talked with Carrie Creemer. Carrie had been horrified. They were socialists, feminists, the oppressive behaviour of someone who purported to understand how women could be dominated by men was so much less forgivable than that of someone who was ignorant. She had started to talk with others in the group. They had asked Orbach to leave.

'It's true. They didn't handle it well. They relied on Alex to deal with Orbach. But Alex couldn't. He never could. He still didn't want to believe bad of him. Orbach could convince him of anything. He was. . . He still is I suppose. . . Brilliant with words. . . Articulate. . . The perfect advocate. . . He could convince you your name was something else, it's a different day, to stand on your head. . .

'Orbach wasn't in chambers much, hardly at all, he was into this inquiry full-time. . . Alex used to go and see him, for lunch, and to help him with his work. . . All the time Alex was seeing him, the rest of chambers thought he was talking it through with Orbach, but actually he was talking about anything but... It's one of his weaknesses, burying his head in the sand... None of the others wanted to see him... I think they were frightened, he'd use that incredible intellect, to win them over... None of them could stand up to him individually...'

So they'd done it collectively instead.

'You're saying, no one asked his side of the story?'

'What side was there? There was nothing to hear. It would all have been lies.'

'Forgive me, Lady Helen... I'm a lawyer... They're lawyers... We're trained to know there are two sides, to hear the other side!'

She shrugged. That was our problem. We were the lawyers. Not her.

'That was why... Someone mentioned an action, legal proceedings... Because of the way they did it?'

She nodded.

A key in the door.

I only had one more question.

Why had she wanted to tell me all this without Alex being present?

When I saw the look on his face, when he walked in and saw me, I had my answer.

He swung on her, livid.

It took all his training to be a gentleman not to start shouting at her in front of me.

Alex Keenan still didn't believe his wife's account of how she came to be found, by their son, in bed with his best friend.

To put it at its simplest, like any good Victorian, caught in the act, she screamed rape.

Keenan helped himself to what was left of the wine and slumped into the sofa.

He still hadn't even said hello.

Then he said:

'Bitterness... A sense of injustice... Perhaps a feeling of betrayal... He built that group with me, more than anyone else... They... No, we... We kicked him out of it, behind his back, when he was bogged down in that damned, damned inquiry and could do nothing about it... He was already exhausted from it, we were already concerned he wouldn't make it through without a breakdown...

'It was cruel. I didn't want it to happen. They were jealous of him, resentful because he contributed so much more to the group than any of them... Perhaps they were jealous because he and I were so close too... It was, I suppose, their one chance to separate us, separate him and me... We were too powerful together... They thought he had too much influence over me... They could do it, through Helen... They used it... But... I let it happen... I was the one person who could have stopped it, told them it was not their business... I didn't. That made me responsible for it. For it all.'

'For four deaths?'

He shook his head fervently:

'I don't believe... Not with all of that... I don't believe he would do this. It wouldn't be Russel. It just wouldn't be him.'

She laughed, and got up, turning on him in scorn:

'You still can't hear a word against him! God, you're so stupid!'

She swung out of the room, slamming the door behind her. Keenan jumped up and followed her out, motioning me to wait where I was. I used the time to examine the airline ticket. It had been used. Keenan had been in Paris while I had been in Oslo.

I held the ticket in my hand, tapping it against the arm of the chair. As I intended, he saw it as soon as he came back in.

I held it out to him without comment.

He shrugged and took it from me.

'Who did you go to see?'

'Someone... A friend...'

'Helga?'

He winced. That told him. Sandy had talked to me. It also must have told him where her loyalties now lay.

134

'I'm not going to tell you, Dave. I won't. . . I won't involve anyone who isn't already involved. . .'

I thought about that last sentence for a moment. It sounded good. Responsible. Serious. It was entirely circular and, as such, utterly without meaning.

'And?'

'And what?'

He had not sat down again. Paced nervously up and down in front of me. .

'And did you get what you went for?'

'I think so, Dave, I think so,' he almost whispered:

'God, I hope so!'

The doorbell rang.

He went to answer it.

A voice most familiar asked:

'Is Mr Woolf here, Mr Keenan?'

I got up to greet my friend.

We stood, the three of us, in the hall.

'Good evening, Mr Woolf. . .'

He was telling me to keep it formal.

'Sergeant. . .'

'I wonder if you'd mind accompanying me, sir. . .'

'Not at all, sergeant. Where are we going?'

'Down to Disraeli Chambers, sir. You see,' he turned to Keenan:

'I'm afraid there's been another death, sir.'

Keenan went as white as the ghost someone as yet unidentified had just become.

He could hardly get the word out:

'Who?'

'Mr Matheson, sir, Mr Henry Matheson.'

Fat Harry.

'Oh, God no. . .'

Then:

'If you're going back to chambers, should I come with you? Can I come with you?'

'I'd rather not, sir, if you don't mind, not at the present, it's not a pleasant sight, sir. . .'

Dowell really didn't like Keenan.

'What do you want me for?' I barked.

'I think you could help us with our enquiries, sir. . .'

He was building up police suspicion, on the premise that it could only increase Keenan's confidence in me.

'I've been here, all evening. . .'

'If you don't mind, sir, accompanying me. . .'

I shrugged and followed him. At the door, as he strode away, I glanced back at Keenan, leaning still against the wall:

'Do you still think you got what you wanted in Paris, Alex?'

It called for no answer. None was forthcoming.

I waited until we had driven away before I grinned:

'How'd'you know I was here?'

He didn't answer.

There were other, more pressing questions that took priority.

He wasn't happy.

I knew why.

He told me without asking:

'No, we didn't catch the cunt.'

I simply couldn't help myself:

'I thought I was supposed to be the one. . .' That couldn't be trusted.

'Can it, Dave. . . I don't feel funny. . .'

'How?'

'Would you believe? Inside. Down the stairs. Broken neck.'

'Fat Harry. . . You know. . . If he did fall. . . He probably would break his neck. . . I mean. . . D'you know what that guy weighed?'

'To the last ounce. It's already in the preliminary report. . .'

'They got scales that big?'

'Nah, you dummy. They cut him into sections and weighed them one at a time.'

He pulled in to the side of the road.

We weren't anywhere near the Temple.

From the glove compartment, he withdrew a hip-flask, and offered it to me first. I wasn't disappointed. Drank deep enough for him to say:

'Don't forget me. . .'

I passed it over.

A tramp hovered outside, looking in the window. He leaned down. Please.

Dowell lowered the screen.

The tramp reached eagerly in.

Dowell grabbed his wrist, ripped it inside the car 'till I heard the old man's head bang on the roof. Then he twisted his arm straight and shoved hard out again. The man fell back against railings, slid to the ground.

I'd been in a similar posture myself. Not that long ago.

Dowell heard my thoughts.

As he wound up the window, he said:

'No. I didn't have to. I'm sorry.'

'Tell him. . .'

'He won't notice. . .'

The sick thing was: he was probably right.

He started the car again.

'You normally get this het up?' Over a death.

'Nope. Just this one. I don't like to be taken for a sucker. . .'

Join the club.

We drove on to the Embankment, and turned illegally right at the bottom of Middle Temple Lane. Like they were tramps, up and over the speed-humps at a speed that shook what was left of my stomach into White Russian.

Inside was littered with policemen, and other officials. For all his lowly rank, they treated Dowell with respect. Even the uniformed inspector spoke as if to a superior.

One of what I guessed was his own men took Dowell aside. Dowell frowned. A quick, heated exchange. His man nodded earnestly. Dowell looked like he could kill.

'I've got to make a 'phone call. I'll be back. Wait here.'

So's I wouldn't get bored, he left me on the landing where Matheson had fallen. It was marked out in chalk. Just like in the movies. Only. A whole bunch bigger.

Dowell was gone ten minutes. Once he got back, he told me the tale.

The chambers' meeting had started at about six thirty. Dowell and his men and women had searched the building. No one else was left in it. The other chambers and doors were all locked. His army had been – as planned – discreetly placed in the basement areas of the other buildings.

Nor had Dowell's calculations disappointed when the members started to leave. Several had as expected gone off in a crowd to the pub. A couple – he didn't tell me which, or even of which sex – left arm-in-arm which was novel gossip but nothing more. Keenan had bounced determinedly out, on his loyal way to the Lady Helen: he alone of them had – as head of chambers – a parking permit, and therefore a car to go home in. That was when Dowell had himself left the site.

Eventually, they were all gone, save Harry Matheson. The remaining two officers were sure they had not missed him. They hardly could. Instead, however, an unknown figure had emerged. It was too dark to get a full description, but they had been sure it was not another, unaccounted member of chambers. They took radio instructions from Dowell, and one of them followed quickly after the stranger, while the other went inside the building.

'He didn't get far. . . The guy went out the right hand alley. My man was behind him. At the corner, someone tripped him up, whacked him pretty hard, left him on the ground, and followed after our target. My man got a good look. There were definitely two. . .'

By that time, the last of Tim's tin-soldiers had found the body.

Dowell led me back out of the building. We walked towards the hall which took up the whole of the end of the courtyard.

'Dinner in progress?'

'Yes.'

The unusual directness of his replies told me I was getting warm. To be on the safe side, I checked:

'The other buildings?'

'Mostly unoccupied. One or two working late. They check out. Nothing.'

'Access?'

He shrugged:

'It seems so. . .'

'How?'

'Come on, I'll show you. . .'

He had the freedom of the Temple that night.

We walked in through the huge oak doors of the dining hall. I had been in such halls before, although not this one. In the entrance, there was a noticeboard, to which were pinned various announcements, including for the dinner that evening.

The dining hall itself was lined with portraits. The good and dead. Pardon me. The good and the dead. Great judges of yesteryear. A few who still sat on the bench. It was a difference without a distinction. Sombre, grey heads, bewigged and bedevilled, spotted with spite, pimpled with prejudice, wracked with wrath, marked by malice.

'Tasty bunch,' I muttered.

'I'd rather have them with me than agin'. . .' Dowell admitted.

'You have,' I reminded him.

The barristers ate at long, school dining-tables, ten or a dozen each side, seated on benches. There were twelve tables in all.

The top of the dining-hall was to the rear of the building. There was a raised platform, on which stood a table longer and wider than those at which mere barristers ate. Around it was arrayed a set of fine, carved, high-backed chairs, with deep red leather seating. That was where the Masters of the Inn ate.

There was a door in the wall behind them. Dowell took me through. Immediately the other side, steps led down, I guessed to the kitchen. The Masters' food would be brought up this way, instead of by the entrance-hall through which came the fodder for the fools at their feet.

Past the steps down, another door led into a lounge of sorts. We were now at the absolute end of the building. The other side of the wall was the courtyard. At the right, I spotted the private facilities. I grinned at Dowell:

'Always wanted to do it somewhere like this.'

I was disappointed. It felt no different.

When I came out, he was slouched tiredly in a deep leather armchair.

I was tired too. I stretched out on a sofa opposite. Without taking off my shoes.

'Careful, ducky, you'll scuff the leather. . .' he said.

'You hate them as much as I do, don't you. . .?'

He didn't answer.

I checked out:

'The kitchen. . . Way through the basements. . . Into Disraeli Chambers?'

'Yup. And no lock on this side. Just a solid, iron bar to lift. . .'

No wonder he was glum.

'They got a guest list?'

Of people who had dined.

'Yes. And no.'

Yes, they had a list.

No, Russel Orbach's name wasn't on it.

'Could. . . Could the man who came through the door have fitted Orbach?'

'Nope. . .'

Could he have been the outside man, who'd helped the murderer get away?

'Nope,' he repeated firmly.

'Have you checked him out yet?'

He shook his head and answered distractedly:

'No grounds. . .'

'That didn't bother you when you decided to come visiting me. . .'

'You ain't a QC. . .'

His heart wasn't in it, though. He was on automatic answerback.

I laid my head against the sofa:

'Who'd ever think a bunch of loony-tunes lefty lawyers were worth the effort! God knows! Even the physical effort. . .'

'That's easy,' he muttered:

'Another loony-tunes lefty. . . You're on the left, Dave. . . Isn't it true? You lot save your real hatred for each other. . .'

There was something in it: when the right are in control, the left only have each other to exercise any power over.

There was something else. In the air. He wanted to tell me. But. He wanted me to guess. I played back the record of the conversation thus far. I came to a gap. Which I wasn't supposed to hear.

'Gimbo. . .'

Bingo.

'I'm not telling you this. . . You understand?'

I waved aside the unnecessary qualification.

'Special Branch. . .'

Political. Strictly political.

I wasn't surprised. I'd been almost there.

An idea was racing round my head so fast I almost couldn't keep up with it, pin it down long enough to say it:

'He was the man outside. He stopped your copper. That's it, isn't it?'

My voice was rising, as if I was afraid of it.

He didn't answer.

He didn't deny it, though.

'But why? For God's sake, why?'

He laughed bitterly:

'Why not, after all? What does he care if someone croaks a lot of commie creeps? They're doing him a favour, really. Him and his mob. Less to keep an eye on, eh?'

'Come on, Tim. . . I can buy that. But why'd he want the one who did it to get away?'

'You have to understand these people, Dave. They're not really part of the police, in the way the public'd understand. They're an institution all on their own. With their own purposes to fulfil.'

I didn't interrupt him to point out he'd used a four-syllable word.

'What they deal in is international. Favours for their opposite numbers. Trading information. Raising debts. It's more important to do a favour for someone, to get them to owe you, than to get a result. Murder. . . They're just not interested. It's a local problem, for local bods like us. . .'

'Yeah, OK, I can dig that. But why actually stop you doing your job?'

'Because. . . Because he wanted to follow him, of course. He's not interested in Disraeli Chambers. He's not even interested in one crazy kraut. . .'

It was the first time he had hinted at the hun-factor in my hearing.

'How'd'you know about that?'

I was getting put out by how little I could learn that everybody else didn't seem already to know.

'I only learned about it today. I did your drum just before I came over here earlier. . . That was how I knew where you'd gone. . .'

'Go on.' I wasn't offended.

'He wants to trace the gang. . . That's all, really. . . That's all there is to say. He'll do anything, screw anyone, to get it.'

'And that was the 'phone call you went off to make? To him?'

He laughed out loud:

'Christ, no. I don't get to speak to him. I spoke to my boss. He suggested we weren't interested in the number two man. What he told me, which wasn't much, tied up with what you've told me.'

'You're guessing, then? What you're telling me is a guess?'

It's funny. I really didn't want to believe it. I'd enough corny sucker faith left in the honour and integrity of the British police not to relinquish the last of it without regret.

'Me? I ain't telling you nothing. I don't know what you're talking about.'

That made two of us.

Chapter Nine

The newspapers had more of it.

A barristers' chambers was the subject of a murder campaign. Five barristers were dead. While two were thought initially to have been accidents, it was now considered virtually certain that they had all been killings. The police were making no comment. Nor was Alexander Keenan, QC, head of the chambers and well-known left-wing lawyer, other than by way of expressions of regret and respect for his dead colleagues.

For once, I felt ahead of the game. Not far. But I knew more than they did. There was no mention in the papers of the German connection. Or of the last Wednesday curiosity. Nor, of course, of Special Branch interest. Dowell's boss was identified as the officer in charge, which was another obvious error. There was no mention of Russel Orbach. That was not so obviously an error. I was still a long way from proving it was an error at all.

I had his offer to see me. Once I could tell him where Keenan had been while we were in Oslo. I now could.

We met at his home. He lived in Highgate, in a ground floor flat. He lived relatively simply, and alone.

'How long have you been here?'

'Four or five years. . .'

'You used to live with Margot McAllister?' The MP.

'Yes.'

The back room was a kitchen-diner, with french windows out to a long garden. There were few other houses in view. A lot of trees; a lot of space. It reminded me of his affection for the Norwegian countryside.

'Nice flat. . . Is the garden shared?'

'No. It's all mine. Nowadays, when houses are converted into flats, the local planning authorities tend to require sharing, so everybody gets a little and no one gets enough. This was an earlier conversion. Come. I'll show you the garden. . .'

From the other end, we looked back at the house:

'Ugly, isn't it?'

He meant the back extension which had made the house large enough to hold three flats, all, he said, as spacious as his own.

'They wouldn't allow that either, nowadays. . . But they'd be right. . .'

Housing, planning, environment – these were his subjects.

'If you don't mind me asking, why did you and Margot McAllister separate?'

He smiled thinly:

'It's not your business. It's not relevant. Since you ask. It was to do with her going into Parliament. . .'

'Because she's Labour?'

'No. Because she's in Parliament. I. . . I like to be left alone, at home . . . I like my space uninvaded. . . An MP is on constant call. . . The telephone doesn't stop, nor the doorbell. . .'

'But. . . You were still together. . . When you broke up with Disraeli Chambers?'

'Ah, I see where you're leading. Yes, we were. But it wasn't because of that. She knew Helen Keenan. We were all very close. To say she was angry, at both of them, would be understatement. Did Helen tell you: that she had long been trying to sleep with me? That she had said so, in front of Margot – and Alex? That I had refused, had not wanted to?'

I shook my head. He knew damn well Helen Keenan would have told me nothing of the sort.

'I don't want you to misunderstand. I'm not particularly proud of what happened. But I was less

responsible for it than her. She had her first chance –
Alex was away, I was drunk, and very, very depressed.
I'd already been contemplating either chucking up the
inquiry, or getting medical help to finish it, before it all
happened. . .

'Did she also tell you: when the kid came down, I
was the one who went up and talked to him, not her?
I spent half an hour or longer with him. We were
talking well. I don't want to say it wasn't traumatic,
but he was fifteen years old, sleeping with girls,
highly intelligent if a little – with parents like that, who
wouldn't be? He understood, he was responsive, it was
a dialogue. . .

'Why, then?'

'A lot of pat phrases come to mind. Some friends
of mine afterwards called her Lady Nolle Tangere. . .
Lady Thou Shalt Not Touch. . . The Untouchable Prin-
cess. . . I wasn't actually supposed to call her bluff.

'Also. . . Over the weekend. . . It happened on a
Friday. . . Before Alex got back, she was calling me
up. . . Calling Margot, too, but Margot had gone away
on the Saturday morning. . . After I had told her, I
hasten to add. . . And I got angry with her. . .'

'Because she was calling you?'

'No. Not at all. Because of what she was saying. It
was all about Alex, and her, and me too if you like.
What a big deal it was. How heavy it might be. As if. . .
It's not easy to explain at this distance. . . But as if she
was trying to turn it into something significant in their
personal lives . . .'

'And was it?'

'On its own, certainly not. Alex and she hardly ever
slept together. She slept around a lot. He didn't care.
He never cared about it. Though the opposite wasn't
true. . . He wasn't allowed to sleep with anyone else. . .
Though he did. . . But, of course, you know that. She
was your partner. . .

'That was one of the things that made it so absurd.
She actually said I did it to get back at him, you know,
to hurt him. But he never was hurt by her screwing

146

around. . . That's part of the point, I suppose. . . She wanted him to mind. . . So she made it something he had to mind. . . Maybe she thought he'd mind if it was me, because I was his best friend. When that didn't work, she claimed rape, because that was something he had to mind . . . If he believed it. . .

'During our few conversations afterwards he was quite emphatic that he didn't care about my having slept with her. . . I wouldn't have let it happen if I'd thought for a minute he would have minded. . .'

'I still don't see why you got angry with her?'

'Because we were grown up, we knew what we were doing, more or less. . . We'd chosen our ways of life, our morals or lack of them. . . We were responsible, and responsible for the consequences, such as they were . . . I was worried about John. . . Though I'd talked to him. . . I knew a reaction was possible, probable even. . . I was worried that we'd hurt him. . . But he was the last consideration on her mind. . . During those calls.

'I didn't express myself very well. I was trying to say that he was the one we should be thinking about, talking about. I put too strongly that I didn't care about ourselves, you know, her, me, Alex. . .'

I saw. Hell hath no fury.

By the time Keenan got back, she had her story ready. She couldn't make a big thing out of an affair with Orbach, because he patently didn't want to know, had made obvious he regretted it had happened at all, not merely or even primarily on account of John, but because he wasn't interested in her.

It doesn't need a degree in psychology to watch it evolve. It had been a misconception. The unthinkable had happened: he had touched her, without adoring her. She had to give an account of it to Alex. Either, it had been her mistake – at least in part, – or, she had no responsibility for any of it. He had done it. Against her will. Rape.

'It's. . . Forgive me. . . But it all seems so petty!'

'Oh, it is. It ought to have fizzled out. But so long

as Keenan wasn't buying her story, she had to find someone else who would. So she went to chambers. She had to make it true in her own mind, by making others believe it. I'd go further than that. I was the only person in the whole world who could positively know she was lying. She had to wipe me out, out of their lives, which meant out of chambers. She knew the jealousy and the hatred of me there. . . She's a clever, manipulative, scheming woman . . . She used them; they used her. . . An unholy alliance.'

He laughed:

'They were so frightened of me. . . I've never really understood why. But, I was in chambers, the evening they were meeting. . . It was a regular, scheduled meeting, we had them the last Wednesday of every month . . .'

I knew. Oh, I did know that.

'Anyway, because of the inquiry I wasn't normally attending, but I happened to be there for half an hour or so at the beginning, to check my post. They knew I was in the building. So, they shut the doors, and whispered behind them. Even when they were all assembled, all together, they didn't dare invite me in to hear what I said. . . They wrote me I was to be asked to leave. . .'

We were sitting by the french windows, inside. He sat with his back to the wall, staring out where none of the nearby houses could be seen. From where I sat, a handful of other properties were in sight – lights on, people in occupation.

His account of the breakup was – if somewhat more full – almost identical with that which Keenan had given me. It was the second time what he said coincided with what one of them said.

'So they got Harry Matheson?'

He turned our talk the way it had to go.

'Who's they?'

'Don't you know yet?'

'Maybe. Do you?'

'In a general sense. . . Yes, of course.'

148

Of course. Orbach the omniscient.

'And why?'

'Yes, that too. You?'

'I know what I've been told. Betrayal. Vengeance. Things like that.'

He smiled. He knew the way I put it could fit the German theme. Or. His own feelings.

'Would you like another drink?'

Throughout our conversation, he had been polite, and mildly spoken. Even when he recounted the tale of the breakup. He lived – of choice – quietly, and alone. He spent his holidays walking or going to museums with an elderly Norwegian lady who he called '*Mor*', meaning Mother. He was a distinguished civil lawyer, who spent his time not shouting down judges or cajoling juries, but calmly advising on fine points of law well out of the limelight.

It should have led me to like, even to trust him.

I had to take one direction or the other.

'Are they right?'

'Meaning?'

'Were they betrayed from Disraeli Chambers?'

'I would say. . .' He chose his words carefully:

'They have reason for what they believe.'

'Are you in touch with them?'

'I have friends. As does Alex. We have some friends in common. . .'

'Which is why you haven't asked me where he was while we were in Oslo?'

'Correct. Did you find out?'

'Yes. Paris.'

'Ah. Not bad. But not good. He went to Paris first. But he didn't stay there.'

'Where?'

He thought for a moment. Whether there was a reason not to tell me. Whether he had a reason for doing so.

'Lyons. His meeting was in Lyons.'

'What did he go for? What did he think he could achieve?'

'He's an advocate. He went to advocate.'

After a minute, perceiving that I had not followed his point, he continued:

'He went to advocate a cessation of hostilities. He went to talk about the left, the need for harmony, to stop tearing each other apart. . . In this case, quite literally. He went to try and convince them Disraeli Chambers had nothing to do with what happened. He could not prove it. It is impossible to prove a negative. He could only urge, and argue and advocate. . .'

'And he failed. . .'

'Yes. He failed. You see, Dave, you know this, you were a lawyer once. . .'

I wasn't sure I liked that. I was still a lawyer. Technically.

'The hardest job for an advocate is when his own case is weak, and he's trying to disguise that weakness, structure his argument around it, hope no one notices. . . It's been my experience you can almost never do it. Perhaps the court or the other side won't be able to identify just what the weakness is, but they can sense that it's there. . .'

Which brought us back to his earlier answer: they had reason for what they believed.

'Where do we go from here?'

He laughed:

'We? I'm going nowhere. . . You seem to have forgotten: I have no objections to what is happening at all. . .'

He spoke as if his attitude was the most natural, or the only reasonable one that someone in his position could adopt.

'Really? You really approve of this, because of what happened? You hate them that much?'

'Yes. Unequivocally yes. They're scum. Hypocritical scum. There's nothing worse than false godheads. They attract a lot of people with the prospect that change is possible, they are different, they can find a way through. Actually, they're the same as those who don't try and change things. . . But the fact that they profess to be different makes them far worse. . .'

'You. . . You were part of them. . . You helped build those chambers. . . Keenan says that, still. . . And. . . You were responsible, for what happened with Helen Keenan. . . However little, however much she was more responsible. . . You had your part in it. . .'

He wasn't angered.

'All true. There's a difference. I meant it. I meant what I said and what I did. Whether we're talking now about politics, law or, if you like, morality. I had my views, my theories, and I said them and acted on them and lived by them and was prepared to take the consequences of them. My mistake was, I thought that was true of the others. . . Actually, it was pure cant, and their behaviour, and her behaviour, was just the same as if we had none of us spent our lives subscribing to particular beliefs. . . You know, Dave, scratch an English socialist and what you find is pure English, the socialism's skin-deep. . .

'There's an old story. A group of Englishmen decide to have a revolution. They form up and march on Buckingham Palace, which they plan to take by force. As they approach, the traffic lights turn red. So, of course, they stop.'

'I don't know. . . I don't know which is more right. A lot of words but restrained action, or carrying the words through into action, regardless of the consequences, in the name of integrity. . .'

'It depends, I think, on values. Human life. Pain and violence. It's painful and violent to kill someone, but it's short and sharp and cathartic in the sense that it often diverts the need to kill others. Or, the other way, involves a lesser pain, less violence, not lethal, spread thin but lasting long.'

I got up to leave: 'Don't you think. . . that it's a good thing we don't have to make those decisions. . . Because. . . gods and governments do it for us. . .'

He didn't answer. He did not like to lie. He did not consider himself bound by the decisions of either.

I had planned to visit Sandy after Orbach. Instead, I went home. I sat on the tube back to Earl's Court profoundly depressed. I was certain of two things. Russel Orbach had not committed the killings. The incident with Helen Keenan had much more to do with it than met the eye.

Ten days had passed since that last chambers' meeting. Getting on for a month since I had seen Mrs Nicholas. I was not surprised to receive a letter from her. I was surprised, however, when she asked me to come to her home.

I spent the night before at Sandy's. She drove me to the station. It had been a good evening, and a better night. On the train, I gave myself a break from Disraeli Chambers. I didn't even prepare what I was going to say when I arrived.

'Mr Woolf?'

The dog-collar would have told me who he was even if I'd never seen him before.

He was such a caricature of the country clergy I expected a beat-up, twenty-year-old Austin for transport. I'd forgotten: the family had money, and plenty of it. I sat instead in the spacious front seat of a Swedish Saab. He drove it like Le Mans.

'I told my wife I wanted to meet you from the train, Mr Woolf. . . She has, of course, told me everything. . . I wanted to form an opinion of you, as it were on my own. . . Do you mind?'

'That depends on what your opinion is. . .'

He liked the answer.

'And what news do you bring us, Mr Woolf?'

I wasn't sure he'd like the next:

'I don't bring us any news, Reverend. I bring it to my client. If she wants to share it with you, that's her decision.' The 'my wife has told me everything' could've been a blind.

'Fair enough. . .'

I'd forgotten. He wasn't the argumentative sort. The lord giveth, the lord taketh away and if the lord don't choose to tell you why you don't holler and scream and bitch about it.

Mrs Nick greeted us at the front door. It was, of course, a big house, for it could not otherwise have accommodated all those barristers, all those years ago. Given recent developments, you would've thought they might've moved somewhere smaller.

We shook hands. Now she was on home ground, she was all mother. None of the hello, how are you and what have you got to say that marked our Harrods tea room sessions. More: make yourself comfortable, you must be tired from the journey, would you like to wash up, we'll have something to eat first.

There were limits on what I could tell them. The Russel Orbach involvement was out of order – I had neither evidence of its relevance nor indeed a rationalization. Just a dash of old-fashioned intuition. I merely mentioned him as someone I had talked with.

Nor, of course, could I so much as hint that the reason Fat Harry's hitman got away was an internal police demarcation dispute. I could say, without lying, that the man had got away: Gimbo had lost him within half an hour.

I did give them more than they could get from the newspapers, though. After all. They were paying me a ton a day, plus expenses, and even The Times only cost thirty pence. I gave them, then, the accredited insider version. The group had got mixed up with revolutionary Germans. Those Germans had been wiped out. Someone connected with them, or possibly a surviving member, was convinced they'd only been caught because of a leak that started at Disraeli Chambers.

I was not surprised that her first question was:

'Was it true?'

'I don't know. It. . . It's generally agreed. . . It may have been. People who. . . get involved with activities of this sort. . . Well, they can learn things. . . They didn't. . . Wouldn't have the caution that those actually

153

participating would have. . . One of them might have been careless. Or. . . Have talked. . .'

'Not Jack, Mr Woolf,' his mother insisted.

The Reverend Nicholas looked more shocked by what he now understood was his wife's prime concern than by the story I had told.

'I said, I don't know. I don't know that they did have information, I don't know if they did leak it, if they did I still don't know who or who to, and I certainly don't know if it was accidental or deliberate. The chances are, we'll never know any of those things. All or most of those who would ever have known for sure are dead.'

'Which suggests. . .' The Rev asserted himself:

'That there would not seem to be much more you can do for us, is there?'

That, of course, was what I had been afraid of.

Mrs Nicholas was disappointed when I didn't come straight back at him with fifty different reasons to carry on. Instead, she did.

'No one has been caught yet. . .'

'The police are involved now. . .'

'What about the other members of chambers?'

'That's not our business, dear.'

'It's still so vague, so uncertain.'

'We know Jack's death wasn't what they said.'

'There are other lines of enquiry, which you could fellow up, aren't there Mr Woolf?' She called for help.

I told you several chapters back. I liked this lady.

'Certainly. For one thing, I am absolutely sure that there are still lines of contact. . . Between them, and people in this country.'

'People who are. . . responsible?'

'No. That's not what I'm saying. But people who are around. I've mentioned a couple of them. Keenan believed he could get through to them. He didn't, of course, as we know. I mean, he didn't succeed in stopping it. But he saw someone. . . Possibly just an intermediary. . . A woman, I think. . .'

'Do the police know about that?'

That was a difficult question. Certainly they knew

Keenan had wanted me out of the way, which meant he was up to something. On the other hand, I had not told Dowell where Keenan had gone, nor had the scribbled notes he would have read in my flat have given him enough to work it out, nor had 'they' – in the shape of Gimbo – managed to keep up with him. Dowell might, of course, already have asked Keenan. He would have been told the same as me. Nothing.

'Why haven't you told them?' he asked.

'I didn't have instructions to do so... From your wife.'

She concealed her smile. She knew me better than that.

'You must tell them, Mr Woolf. Mustn't he, dear?'

'I don't know. What do you think, Mr Woolf?'

It was the first time I had been forced to ask myself why I hadn't told Tim Dowell that part of the conversation with Keenan. Or, indeed, when Sandy had said it to me the day after I got back from Oslo.

'You have to follow through the consequences. If I tell that to the police, they will be bound to do something about it. They'll have Keenan in. The papers may get hold of it. Let's suppose, and it's a fair guess, he won't tell them who he saw, and where. Then the issue becomes barrister withholding information in murder hunt. Keenan's under a different pressure, outside pressure, pressure that's got little or nothing to do with what happened in the past, but is all about his present conduct. It seems to me, well, that that would be less productive...'

'Than what, Mr Woolf?'

'Than leaving him where he is... Sweating... About what he knows, and what he hasn't told anyone...'

The Reverend Nicholas took one last shot:

'But he might tell them... He might tell them even though he wouldn't tell you. After all, they are the police.'

She answered for me:

'Exactly, dear. Think of Jack... Think of what Jack would have done...'

I swear he muttered something unsaintly underneath his breath. All he said out loud though was, resignedly: 'It's your decision. . . Dear.'

The way he said 'dear' wasn't that different from the way I'd said it to Sandy a couple of times in the not too distant past.

Sandy was at the station. It hadn't been arranged.

'You waited here all this time?'

'You flatter yourself. . . get in.'

I waited to be told.

She waited to be asked.

I'd played this game before.

With someone I didn't like.

Lady H.

The comparison didn't help and I was glad this time it was she who broke first.

'In the back of my mind. . . You remember talking about Helga?'

I was hardly likely to forget.

'I had an old file, of miscellaneous papers, from those days. . . Minutes, and the odd letter, and leaflets. . . That sort of thing. It was in our dead-file room. . .'

All solicitors have a store for their closed cases. You never know, for sure, if something might go live again.

'Filed under what?'

'A pile of other junk,' she answered, knowing that wasn't what I meant.

'What have you got?'

'Her name. Helga Schroeder. It's stupid. Because I should have remembered. The psychologist's daughter.'

Sandy had done a degree in psychology, at University College in London, before she had studied to become a solicitor.

'This Schroeder. You know where to reach him?'

She laughed:

'He was dead before I ever met her.'

'How come you didn't remember the other night?'

156

'It wasn't a big thing, meeting her. Just at the end of a meeting, I caught her name. I said: any relation? she said yes, and I should think was fairly embarrassed. He was very right wing. I mean, bordering on the Nazi. After the war, he was imprisoned in France. And for some years after, he had worked at a hospital in Lyons. It was when you mentioned Lyons last night, the penny began to drop. . . So I went looking for the file. I didn't say anything, in case it didn't turn out,' she added, anxious as ever to allay any residual mistrust.

'Not bad,' I conceded.

We went back to her house. I was beginning to spend more time there than at home. The food was better. I didn't have to clean up.

I had a name. I also had a place. I made one 'phone call – to clear the expenditure – and another – to book the ticket. The next afternoon, I was on a plane for France.

Only once I got there did I begin to wonder where to start looking. Another needle in another haystack. But Lyons – unlike some of the other parts of London where I had been scavenging – was too pretty to burn down.

I wasted three days asking questions to which I got no useful answers.

'Are there many Germans here?'

'Where do they go to?'

'Did an Englishman called Keenan stay in your hotel?'

'Are there many left-wing groups in this town?'

'Where do they gather?'

'Has a German woman called Schroeder stayed in your hotel?'

'Did you serve dinner to an Englishman accompanied by a German woman?'

I even followed a few lithe, blonde women, on the somewhat less than sophisticated grounds that the French were Latins and accordingly ought to be dark-haired and darker skinned.

I was contemplating two unpleasant courses of conduct. I could call up Dowell, tell him where I was, and get him to OK co-operation from the frog pigs. Or. I could go home with less to show for it than I brought back from Norway.

Then I had a brainwave. The sort of idea that made me worth every penny of the hundred pounds a day I was being paid.

Sandy had said Helga's father used to live in Lyons.

I looked in the telephone directory.

All good things come to those who waste their time and their client's money.

I took a taxi straight there.

No one at home.

I sat inside a café across the road, sipping *café noir* and *pastis* alternately until my palate couldn't tell the difference between them.

I tried again when it was dark and good Germans should be honouring the curfew. Still no answer.

I couldn't drink any more so I settled down to *stek-frites*. The meat was, though thin, tender, and the chips fried crisp. I had moved on to *vin rouge*, because I didn't know how to ask for anything else, but watered down with Perrier. I was well into my second glass when a woman entered the café, and came and sat down at my table without a moment's hesitation.

She snapped at me in French.

'*Nicht sprechen französisch*,' I utilized what was left of a one year course in German during my childhood, liberally seasoned with Yiddish.

'You don't speak German very well either, do you?' she said in perfect English.

'I came to France once, with a few friends. On one of those day trips, shopping expeditions you know? The boat was French. One of them went up to the bar and ordered for us. When he came back, he said to his girlfriend how pleased he was to find he hadn't forgotten the language. She said: "You'd break into Swahili if the alternative was silence".'

'I don't understand,' she frowned.

158

I'd forgotten. Krauts ain't got no sense of humour.

'It doesn't matter. I'm the opposite. I can't speak any language but English, and even that's not my own. . .'

'Where are you from?'

I always do this, whenever I meet a German:

'I'm a Jew. . .'

'With a hatred of Germans. Yes. That is all right. Now. What do you want?'

'I want to talk to you.'

'We are talking.'

I glanced around, to indicate that there were people at nearby tables.

'The French consider it beneath their dignity to hear anything but their own language, too. . .'

'It's. . . confidential,' I still wasn't comfortable:

'And you're the one who didn't open your door when I came up. . .'

That was a guess. That she had been inside at least at my second try and watched me cross back over to the café. She didn't contradict me.

'I do not know you. What is your name?' She was obviously a well brought up lady. You don't take someone into your home at least until you know his name. Even if killing them's a possible way to pass the evening.

'Dave. Dave Woolf. We haven't met. But. We might have. We used to go to the same places, we have some shared acquaintances. . .'

'In London?'

'Yes. We used to go to the same type of meetings. . . At places like Disraeli Chambers. . . And our acquaintances include Alex Keenan. . .'

She didn't bat an eyelid. By this time, I figured, she had worked that much out for herself.

'Perhaps I do not know who is this man?'

She had also figured out: I wasn't police, I had no clout, she didn't need to be afraid of me.

'I didn't say he was a man. . .'

It might've been short for Alexandra.

She threw her face up in a classic – if adoptive –

French gesture of dismissal. If that was the best I could do.

'Still you have not told me what you want.'

She was hard. She was not going to budge.

'I would like to meet someone. I think you know how I can do that. I want to meet them and talk to them. I am not police, I promise to tell nothing to the police, there's things I need to know from this person. He can say where, when, in what country and what conditions. But. I must meet him.'

She thought for a moment.

Then. She asked:

'What is his name?'

I shook my head from side to side, slowly:

'I do not have a name. Please. Get him my message. Ask him.'

'Where are you staying?'

I gave her the name of the hotel.

She rose.

'Perhaps,' she paused.

Then she added, but clearly in a different sentence.

'I might want to know where you are staying so that I can complain to the police that you are pestering to me.'

I shrugged.

What the hell. Everybody else did. Why shouldn't I?

'You will see.'

Only. She was gone. So I didn't.

I had to wait forty-eight hours. She would take her time. Make sure neither I nor anyone else was following her. I did not know if she would be making contact with him in person, or by telephone. But the flics didn't come calling on me.

I spent a lot of the time walking, anywhere but near her apartment. I even took in a couple of movies I'd wanted to see in London but not had the time for. One of them was, as I had assumed, subtitled. The other was dubbed into French. I only stayed five minutes. I ate a lot, and decided red wine wasn't that bad for me after all. I'd say: Lyons is one of the towns I now know my way about best of all.

She caught up with me as I was out walking, on the bridge, beginning to think the shot hadn't paid off.

'Do you have an answer for me?'

'Yes.'

'And?' I almost grabbed her in my eagerness.

'Go home, Mr Woolf. Just go home.'

'What is that? No? Or. . . Wait there?'

She shrugged: it was an infectious habit.

'You send a message. I bring an answer. It is: go home. That is all.'

I looked at her.

She stared right back.

She was hard as nails.

She said:

'I hope you have a pleasant flight. . .' And was gone.

Chapter Ten

We passed into a new phase of killing. Killing time.

It was mid-month. The inner circle, those in the know, anticipated no activity for another couple of weeks.

The police, however, could not afford to take chances. Each and every surviving member of the group, willing or not, was accompanied at all times of day and night by an officer of the law. It was, of course, a guarantee that no German would come near them and, as such, an assurance that we stood not a chance of catching anyone actually in the act.

Anne Godwin's spectre of a fast-disappearing practice had become a reality, though not quite for the reasons she had expected. While the officers were prepared to wait outside rooms in which conferences were being held, the sight of six feet of silver and blue politely holding open the door was enough to deter most of their criminal clientele.

This period marked, and this activity reflected, a decline in the fortunes of the only member of Her Majesty's Constabulary I had ever, albeit only fleetingly, termed friend.

It would be fair to say that he had not exactly covered himself with glory the night of the Matheson massacre. (I appreciate that a massacre normally denotes the death of many. You didn't know Fat Harry like I knew Fat Harry. Bodyweight made it an appropriate term.)

In addition, as Dowell had so carefully not told me

before he disappeared from the scene, there were those on high who did not share his sense of priorities.

He was not taken off the case altogether. Insultingly, he was given the task of co-ordinating the duty roster of bodyguards.

'Do I detect the kindly hand of the gormless Gimbo behind this move?' I asked on one of our outings to the all-night caff with so many differences.

'Gimbo. . . As you choose to call him. . . And, of course, were I to admit he existed. . . Is a four-eyed get with wrinkled walnuts for bollocks . . .'

There was one major drawback to the increased frequency of these occasions. Lewis had implied that if we didn't start at least occasionally paying for our liquor, he'd show us a variation on water into wine. To wit. Southern Comfort into cold soda.

Tim Dowell could hardly put in for expenses.

Which left.

Me.

We were keeping company for the same sort of reason that Marguie Bradkinson had claimed she wanted me to go with her to Oslo. We were participants in the same performances. Only. The curtain had got stuck and the show couldn't yet go on.

He tossed his – Mrs Nick's – drink to the back of his throat.

'You're a greedy pig, Dowell,' I remarked boredly, for want of anything even vaguely interesting to say.

'Probably. . . I told you before. It's a pig job. Pig world. Pig people . . .'

'You sound like Orbach. . .'

'You're obsessed by him. . . There's not a jot of evidence he's got anything to do with it. . .'

'Agreed. Not evidence. But. I know he is.'

'I'll tell you why you think that, if you like,' as casually as if inviting me to buy another round.

'Go on. . .'

'You think you're him. Or he's you. . .'

'Wha. . .?'

'The way I see it. You're both lawyers. You've both

163

got pissed off with ... What did you call them the
other night? Loony-tunes lefties. . . You're both Jews,
too. . .'

'What's that got to do with it?'

'Quite a lot. You're both outsiders. You don't feel
you really belong. It's hard work for you to go on
belonging.'

'Belonging to what?'

'It doesn't matter really. Whatever you seem to
belong to. In this case, groups, your profession. . .
He quit Disraeli Chambers. . . You quit your job. . .
It's easier for you to do that. Get out. Become the
outsider you think you are anyway. That's what you've
got in common. But that's all . . .'

'He didn't quit. . . He was pushed. . .'

'You can make it happen. . . To yourself. . .'

'They teach you psychology at police college nowadays?'

'As a matter of fact, yes. But not that.'

'Where'd'you get it from?'

'From a book. . .'

'I didn't know you could read,' I bantered for time to
absorb what he'd said. There was more than nothing in
it. He hadn't spelled out why this alleged identity crisis
should lead me to suspect Orbach of an involvement
beyond that of merely keeping himself informed. It was
implicit. If I had been in his position, I feared I might
have wanted to do something similar.

'Oh, yes, I read comics, and pin-up magazines. . .
And a book called Resistance to Conforming. . . You
ever read it?'

I shook my head.

'It's by a man called Schroeder. A professor of
psychology. A German.'

I shut my eyes.

To give me time to think.

It had not come from anything I had written down.
Since his last confessed unscheduled visit to my home,
I had been taking precautions. I had written notes.
Because I needed to write things down to clear my
head. At the end of the day, I was either going to write

a damned full report for Mrs Nicholas or a novel about the whole incident or both.

So I did not and could not burn them eat them swallow them chew them tear them into tiny pieces and flush them down the loo. Instead. I posted them. To their eventual owner. The aforementioned Mrs Nick. Not to read. But to keep safely for me. She had been getting them. She had told me so. Not in an obvious way, by mail or phone. In the code I had devised and which I had suggested she use to indicate safe receipt.

'Gimbo?'

'I told you before. He and I ain't on talking terms. No. So far as I'm aware, he knows nothing.'

'Why?'

'Why what?'

'Why haven't you told him anything?'

'Because the only people who know are you and me. And, I would have thought, that was already one too many. . .'

'You still haven't told me how you found out. . .'

'No more I have.' He sighed:

'I suppose I ought?'

'You suppose right.'

'I opened up your girlfriend's office last night. My, she's thorough, notes of everything. . .'

'Do you even begin to understand that the way you keep pilfering people's premises without a warrant is unlawful unconstitutional *ultra vires* unethical unpalatable and unpleasant?'

'What was the Latin bit in the middle?'

If he recognized it as Latin, he didn't need an answer.

'Oh, fuck it, Tim. . . Why're you telling me?'

'You're wrong, you know. . .'

'What's wrong?'

'All those fancy words you used. All the law says is you can't use what you find in evidence. That's different. Isn't it? It doesn't mean I can't know about them. . . I suppose, thinking about it, it might be a little bit of trespass. . . But I never harm anything, or anyone, and I never take anything so it isn't criminal

165

damage or burglary. Right, Mr Woolf? So sue me in a civil court. . .'

I sighed. I didn't even bother to ask what would happen if I reported him. He knew I wouldn't. Nor, if she gave a damn about me, would Sandy.

'What are you going to do with the information?'

'Not much more than I have already.'

'Which is?'

'Reading the collected works of the aforesaid father. . . That's what Sandy's note says: Helga, Schroeder's daughter. . . Then the name of this book sort of not written on the note, more like a doodle around it.'

'She studied psychology. . . At college. . .'

'Oh. I wanted to do that. I did law instead.'

'You. Did law. At university.'

By the end of the sentence, though, my voice had ceased to show surprise. It explained a lot.

'How come you're only a sergeant?'

'Oh, I've got my inspector's exams. Had them for years. But, well, it's a sort of positive discrimination in the force. In favour of idiots. They make a lot of fuss about wanting it to be more of a graduate profession, and they send a dozen or more inspectors or chief inspectors to university each year, to get a degree, usually law, sometimes sociology. . . But they're the only ones that really do well out of being educated. . . They've already shown they can stomach the mass stupidity. . . Anyone like me – and there are few, very few – who've got an education beforehand, well, we have to prove ourself, work really hard to show it won't get in the way. . .'

While he was talking, I was thinking. All he'd got was a name. Helga Schroeder. He would, of course, have to be even more crass than the average copper he'd now admitted he wasn't not to connect her with the German gremlin in our game. But he'd said he was going to do nothing with the information. Which meant he had appreciated for himself that she was not the person we were actually after.

166

'Let me think out loud. Just to show I didn't waste my expensive education either. . . You know she ain't the one we want. . . Right?'

'I'd a fair idea. . . She's what? A contact? Who Keenan went to see?'

'Agreed. And abroad.'

'Yes. . .' He'd worked that out too.

'So if you do anything with it, you have to work abroad. . . Which means giving it to Gimbo?'

'Not necessarily. But the effect would be the same. Once it goes on to the circuit, outside the country, his type will be involved. If not him immediately, it'll filter back to him.'

'Which means action maybe gets taken abroad. . . Which means not here. . . Which means maybe not for these murders but. . . But what?'

'I don't honestly know. But I'd think, with some idea of what sort of people we're talking about, terrorists, international networks, you've read it all in the papers. . . We'll clock in somewhere about ninety-ninth in the list of people wanting a piece of him. . .'

'Why does it matter to you, Tim? You can't bring them back. . . It brings it to an end. . . So?'

He laughed:

'Buy me a drink. . .'

'Another?'

'I'm an outsider too, Dave. . . In my own way. . . In my own scene. . . In the police. Educated copper. What a joke. What a lot of jealousies. What a lot of obstacles placed in my way. I've often thought, it must be like what being black or Jewish is like. . . Oh, not so difficult, and I can always change, by getting out. . . There were Jews at my school. We used to give them a hard time. That was before the blacks came, of course. It was the best break your lot ever had. . .'

'Thanks for nothing, I'd left school by then. . .'

'It's not important. I just wanted you to know I do have some idea of what prejudice is. . . In my own little way, in my own little world. . . God, the amount of times I've walked into a new station, ready to be one of the lads. . . Only to be greeted by the station sergeant: "So you're the college boy, eh, well we'll soon knock that out of you. . ." Or some similar such shit. . . I could understand it if I was throwing myself about a bit, you know, putting them down, showing off. . . But I learned not to do that early on, and I'm not bad at hiding it now. . .'

'Jesus. She's paying me a ton a day for some copper to cry on my shoulder?'

'Right,' he grinned, brought back to the point:

'Because if I follow it up that far. . .' He held up his thumb and forefinger as if indicating – a drink this size:

'There's no way I could bring it back home. Even if we find him on English soil, with what we've currently got, he'll be out of the country before you can whistle the Red Flag. . . And. . . And I want the bastard here. Not there. Here.'

'Which is the bit that matters: here, or that you want to be the one to get him?'

'Maybe both. . . Maybe, just maybe. . . I make no admissions, you see. . . But maybe I don't want to read he tripped down the cell stairs in some German goal, or committed suicide like the rest of that mob were supposed to have done. . .' Another unbeliever:

'And maybe I don't really care about international terrorists and the like. Maybe I think that's abzll over my head, there's too many ifs and buts and pros and cons and all the rest of it. . . So I'm better off out of it. . . I don't want to be in Special Branch, I don't want to get involved in that. Just policing the community. . . That's the phrase nowadays, isn't it? That's for me. . .'

'Don't you care, if all he'll do is twenty, thirty years, for what. . .five lives now?'

'Do you believe in topping?'

'No. I thought you would. I thought all policemen did.'

I realized what I'd said, and laughed out loud:

'What was that word you used? Prejudice?'

'Something like that. No, I don't really care. . . He's what, thirty? He's got to be thirty, now or not far short, if he's paying off a debt that old. . . He goes to prison for twenty years. Comes out he's fifty, maybe more: the court'll probably stick a minimum recommendation on him. What do the new rules says?'

'I don't know. But twenty years sounds likely. . .'

'So, he's fifty and he's too old to get a job, start again, he won't even know anyone or have anywhere to go. . . Everyone will have forgotten him . . . All your radicals who'll think he's some kind of hero or martyr. . . And will they? If what he's done for is murdering this mob?'

'What I said the other night. . . You don't really like them, do you?'

'Nah. . .'

'Why?'

He shrugged:

'Who needs a reason? Would you buy a used wig from one of them? No, I don't like them. It's not 'cos they're left-wing or help the poor. . . The whole idea, of lawyers, professing to be on the side of the oppressed. . . It's a contradiction, isn't it? The only people they've liberated is themselves, financially, intellectually. . . Making sure there's always an oppressed class is essential to them. . . It's what they get their living from. . .'

'What about the clients? Don't they matter? Does it matter if people pretend they're doing something special, something political, if they're also making positive gains, in individual lives? If they didn't have the politics, they'd probably end up in commercial work or city firms screwing every last penny they could out of the system, and to hell with the wee people's problems. It's just their way of convincing themselves to do that particular job. . .'

I don't know why I was defending them. Maybe because what he said was also true of many years of my own life.

'There's a lot of good, sympathetic lawyers, who do a

169

good job, like that, without making all the noise about it. . .'

'I think that'd probably qualify as another Orbach line. . .'

'The difference is, between me and friend Orbach, and assuming there's something in what you believe. . . All I've said is, I don't like them. I don't go around wanting to see their heads chopped off. . .'

'I thought it was me was supposed to be like Orbach?'

'I said that's what you think. I didn't say you were. I told you what you've got in common. I said that was all. . .'

'Maybe. . . Maybe not. . .'

'Maybe, friend Woolf,' he said quietly: 'Maybe that's what you've got to decide. . . Which you do want to be: him or me. . .' he grinned: 'What a terrible choice in life. . .'

I'd been back from Lyons four days when I got the first call. It was from a coin box. It was seven thirty in the evening.

'Mr Woolf?'

'Yes. . .'

The voice was accented.

So I wanted to believe.

I was so keyed up I couldn't be sure.

Even after his next sentence:

'Take the M4. Drive to Newbury. Find a street. It is called Wendon Way. Park outside number 100. Wait there. Do it now. Be alone.'

He hung up before I could tell him. I don't have a car.

I rang Sandy at home. She wasn't in. Just her damned answering machine. I got as far as her cheerful but unoriginal 'hi' before I put the receiver down. Then I called her office. There was no reply, of course, from the switchboard. I dug her private number out of my book. No reply. I cursed, replaced the receiver again and was wondering how the hun would feel if I turned up in a minicab when my own phone rang.

170

'Did you try to get me just now?'

'Oh, Sandy, oh yes I did! Why didn't you answer?'

'I was on the loo. . . I picked it up on your last ring. . . Are you coming over?'

I'd forgotten a tentative date.

'Oh, no. Listen. You have to do something for me. Can you come here. Right now. In the car. Lend it me. It's urgent, Sandy, I wouldn't ask, but. . .'

She hesitated for about five seconds. Then, she said yes.

I spent the time I had to wait on bended knee. Praying. First in thanks for Sandy's existence. Secondly that she wouldn't have an accident on the way over. Thirdly that I'd be safe in Newbury.

I'd double locked the door and was standing upstairs on the pavement by the time she arrived. Held the door of her car open for her. She said:

'I'll come with you. . .'

I think she expected the answer, because she didn't put up much of a fight. She got out, leaving the keys in the ignition, and stood to one side while I slid into the driver's seat and adjusted my distance from the pedals, the rear-mirror, the wing-mirror.

'How's this work?' I pointed.

'Push the tape in first. That switches it on. Then adjust the volume. It comes out on its own at the end. You don't have to switch it off. There's an automatic cut-out.'

'Right. . .'

I turned the key. The petrol indicator rose jerkily to the top. She had filled it on the way over. I glanced at her and she nodded in confirmation. I took the hand-brake off and started to pull out.

'Hey,' she called:

'Don't you have anything to say to me?'

'Like?'

'Like thank you? Like where you're going? Like when you'll bring it back? Like do I want to wait for you and would I like the keys to your flat? Like have I got the cabfare home?'

I thought about it. Lot of questions. I muttered my answer:

'I'm beginning to think you're all right, kid. . .' and drove off with her yelling after me:

'What? What did you say?'

That was a close call. She'd nearly heard me. I had to get a grip on myself. Within a hundred yards, I was beginning to make sense again.

Have you ever driven into a strange town, in the middle of the evening, with nothing more than a street name to tell you where to go? It ain't easy. As a matter of fact, Newbury ain't that easy to find at all, once you get off the motorway. But. I made it to the town centre, before I stopped the car, got out and – like I was taught when I was a child – asked a copper where Wendon Road was. He had to radio in to find out. That took another five minutes. Then he explained. Not once. Because I can't follow street directions. Three times. Before I was ready to take a shot at finding it.

Inevitably, it was outside the town centre, back the way I'd just come.

It was after ten by the time I had Wendon Way, and the right number house. They're pretty houses. Detached. Lot of distance between each driveway. There were no lights on in the front of number 100.

I sneaked in and peered through what turned out to be the kitchen window. There were lights at the back of the house. After a couple of minutes, a tall, slender, gracefully grey-haired, bespectacled woman came in, and started to make a hot drink. She looked about as German or gangster-like as Captain Furillo's lady-lawyer-wife on Hill Street Blues.

I settled down to wait in the car. Sandy didn't have no Wagner, so I put some Mahler on the tape-deck, to make him feel right at home. After half an hour, I switched to Beethoven, my fifth. He was German too. We might as well both be happy.

Still no show. The lights started to go off, one by one, in the house. I figured. What the hell. I walked straight round to the side where the front door was and rang. I heard the lady call out in a strong northern accent:

'James. There's someone at the door.'

A bespectacled man of about seventy, with white hair and a sharp white beard, wearing an artist's smock, opened up, wielding a paintbrush like a weapon.

'Yes?' He asked, curious but polite:

'Can I help you?'

'My name's Dave Woolf. . .' I answered.

He thought about this for a moment.

'Yes,' he said again:

'Is that with an e or without?'

'Without. And two os.'

He nodded wisely:

'That's the second most common spelling. I knew a family who spelled it with one o, and no e on the end. That's most unusual. I don't suppose. . . Well, no, hardly, you wouldn't, would you. . .'

I saw his point. I might as well be called Smith as be related to his friends the Wolfs.

From upstairs his wife called:

'James?'

'Coming Marjorie. . . It's a mistake, I think. . .' He turned to me:

'It must be, really, if you spell it with two os. Don't you think? We can't stand here chatting all night. Good night. It has been most pleasant.'

He didn't wait for my answer, but shut the door firmly in my face.

I had to agree. It did seem to be a mistake.

I waited until one o clock before I gave up and drove back to town.

I had three choices. I could drive straight home and sort the car out the next day. That was the most convenient course of action for me. Or. I could drive to Sandy's, and post the keys through her letterbox. That would certainly be the most convenient for her.

I compromised. I drove to Sandy's, and rang the bell long and hard enough for her to come and let me in.

'Have a nice drive, dear?' she asked sarcastically.

173

'Certainly. I met a charming man who once knew some people called Wolf who spelled their name with only one o, but no e on the end. . .'

She absorbed this slowly. It was quite a lot to take in at nearly three o clock in the morning.

Obviously, it was more than she could cope with. She trotted back to bed, leaving the door open so I could see her climb into·bed. She sat up, and pulled her nightdress off, adjusting her position so she was clearly only taking up half the bed. Leaving the other half pointedly vacant.

I sighed. I was tired. Dog tired. Like I couldn't hardly walk. She wasn't inviting me to go for a walk.

That was how we were engaged when her phone rang.

'I don't believe this,' she murmured as she extracted herself from underneath me and padded off to the living room to take the call.

She stood in the doorway:

'It's for you. . .dear,' the last word was wearing a little thin.

'Didn't happen to say who, by any chance?'

I'd've put money on Dowell. Roster organizer or not.

'Mr Woolf,' the same voice as before:

'It would seem. . . You were not accompanied to Newbury. . .'

He hung up.

Having thus communicated to me two things.

That the purpose of the exercise was to see if I did go on my own.

That he had been following me. And knew where I now was.

We both sat up in bed, clutching our knees.

'How did he know my number?'

'I was about to ask that. . .'

'So? Answer already. You're the detective. . .'

'I'll give seven possibilities. One, he took the number of the car and told a policeman it had scraped his. They're not supposed to help out this way, but if they don't you'll pretend you want to prosecute, just to find out who it is. So they have to go through a lot of paperwork that's wasted. Instead, they'll usually get you what you want over the radio. . . Which is: name and address, enough to look the number up in the telephone book. There's a problem with it. It takes a hell of a lot of familiarity with the system here. . .'

'It's not bad, though. . . How'd'you know about it?'

'I used to do it for our clients. Pretend I'd been in an accident myself, you know, ask the nearest copper I could find. . .'

'Maybe coming back to work isn't that good an idea. . .'

With ethics like mine, I could get us both struck off.

'It got results,' I protested. I still hadn't told her, and didn't like to tell her, it wasn't a patch on some of the methods adopted by Sergeant Dowell.

'What are the others?'

'Orbach told him. Keenan told him. You told him. Dowell told him. Gimbo told him. How many's that?'

'Five – six in all – and one of them I didn't like. . .'

She waited for an apology.

I climbed from the bed and stared out the back. It looked on to her garden. For all I knew he could be waiting there.

'Sorry,' I mumbled.

'What was the seventh?'

'Oh, easy. . . Someone we haven't thought of yet. . . You know: the surprise answer at the end of the book. . .'

I got back into bed and put my arm around her.

She pushed it away, roughly.

'Hey, I said I'm sorry. . .'

'Listen, Dave. I heard what you said in the car. . .'

Shit. The trouble Disraeli Chambers were in was as nothing.

'And, you know, you're behaving like a complete arsehole. . . Just like you used to. . . I don't want that. If you want to be with me you trust me and that's fine and you're right to and let's lie down and cuddle up and maybe more. . .

'If you don't trust me, don't give me any crap. Just get your clothes on, get the hell out and don't bother coming back. You know? I haven't done everything smart in my life either. . . But I'm not going to make the same mistakes twice over. . .'

What could I say to a speech like that?

'But. . . Sandy. . . It's four o'clock in the fucking morning and it's freezing out there!'

She swung on me like she was about to tear my eyes out. Then she saw the way I was looking at her. And burst out laughing, and hugged me instead.

Yeah. I trusted her. After all. I didn't seem to have a lot of choice. I'd gone too far with her already for it to make any difference. It'd just be cutting off my nose to spite myself.

For want of anything better to do while I awaited my next call, I rang Dowell with the number of Sandy's car and asked him to check if it'd been the subject of a radio accident enquiry the night before. Negative. That narrowed the options down. To six. Or, rather, five. Of which one was anyone's guess.

I didn't like this marking time. I wasn't good at it. I felt like a prize race-horse, or a football player, when rain cancels game at the very last moment. Chomping at the bit. I was so jumpy, I even hung out at Sandy's office, drawing up formal bills for clients from the notes on case-files. It was always one of the jobs I was better at. Gave me that little chance for some creative writing.

He played me for a sucker again. This time it was Brighton. I nearly refused to go at all. My father came from Brighton. You know how I felt about him. I had to wait at the end of the West Pier, in the freezing cold, with next to no one else about, and all of the arcades shut up for the season. All I got out of it was a stick of rock Sandy chipped a tooth on and didn't thank me for.

I wondered. How come you never read about this

part of it in thrillers? How come you never see it on Hill Street Blues? I knew the answer, because it was exactly what I felt like doing: putting the book down, or switching off.

The third time he rang, also from a call box, right after he opened with his unvarying introduction:

'Mr Woolf.'

I butted in.

'This time had better be for real 'cos I ain't playing any more. Geddit?'

It sounded good, I thought, as I listened to the dialling tone. The sucker had hung up on me.

Thirty seconds later, there was a rap at my door. He was standing there, carrying a holdall. He must have called from the phone box in the square. I was more surprised it was working than to see him.

He pushed past me, slamming the door shut behind him, and poking his head into room after room until, satisfied, he settled down at the table beneath my bed platform. He was still clutching the handle of his bag.

He was not as I had imagined him. He was thicker set, and darker haired. His face was heavily pock-marked. He wore glasses. But at least they were rimlessly revolutionary. I put him at about my own age. Nearer forty than thirty.

'I suppose it'd be idle to ask your name?'

He smiled.

Ye gods. A hun with a humour.

'Don't you think. . . Well. . . It's a little risky here? I mean, it's a basement, there's no way out, you know.'

'Should I not trust you, Mr Woolf?'

'Trust, shmust. . .' There I went again.

'I don't know, man. I don't know what that means. I haven't told anyone. You've followed me to Newbury and Brighton and my girlfriend's and God knows where. . .'

'Everywhere, Mr Woolf. For the last few days, everywhere. . .'

'Well, you're better at it than Special Branch. I spotted their man the first day I was tailed. . .'

As I said it, I realized I didn't know if it was true, how long Gimbo had been up my backside before I picked him up on the tube home from the Angel.

'They are not so good, the British police. . . I think. . . Perhaps. . . They do not have the experience of those in my country. . . Perhaps. . . They do not take it so seriously. . .'

Christ. Another damned philosopher. Next thing he'd be telling me it was all because Britain had never been invaded by a foreign power.

'Some of them are good. . . Perhaps better than you think. . .' I had Dowell in mind, not Gimbo.

'It is possible.' He placed his holdall on the table. From it he extracted what looked to my television-trained eye suspiciously like a sub-machine gun.

I glugged silently.

When I was at public school, we had cadet training. We went on a camp once, to somewhere on Dartmoor. It was the miserablest two weeks of a pretty miserable childhood. The only good moment was when we got to play with sub-machine guns. Only. They didn't look anything like the one he had placed in front of him on my table. The difference was between the Wright Brothers' Flying Machine and Concorde.

(This is totally irrelevant. Before I took my turn, they forgot to change the target. Accordingly, they couldn't score me. Instead of wasting more ammunition, the soldier in charge wrote me down as 100%. With a sub that's an impossibility. He didn't give a damn: It was just school kids, and no one would believe it anyway. It gave me my one credit for the course: I got to be the only guy in recorded military history who scored nothing but bullseyes with a sub-machine gun. Even Clint Eastwood couldn't've.)

'You wanted to talk with me, Mr Woolf. . .'

Now I'd got what I wanted, I couldn't remember half the questions I'd started off with.

What I really wanted to do was just gaze. I'd never been involved in a murder case – even as a solicitor. I'd never seen a murderer before. Not in real life.

Flesh and blood. Also. This guy had whacked off five barristers whom I knew. He had run rings round me and Dowell and the British Special Branch and presumably the German police and just about everybody else you could think of. He'd earned me my first real bread for what seemed like many years. He'd got me out of a gutter in which I looked like drowning. He'd incidentally set me up in my first affair for longer that I cared to recall. And. He was sitting in my flat as calm as you please, resting his hand on a sub-machine gun. I mean. Just how kitsch can you get?

Chapter Eleven

I sat in the waiting-room of Malcolm Harryngton's chambers, with only two thoughts to keep me company. One was I was spending a hell of a lot of time buzzing around barristers these days. It was a pain in the butt. As Sandy said, if that was what I was going to do, I might just as well be back in practice. (No. She had not given up that most crazy of all her ideas.)

The second was marginally more particular. Of all the barristers I had recently been to call on, only Harryngton had kept me waiting. Keenan hadn't. Orbach hadn't. It did not endear him to me.

I had met Harryngton before, years and years before. In the earliest days of practice, in my enthusiasm, I had joined an organization which went by the less than catchy title of the Progressive Lawyers Campaign, inevitably and invariably abbreviated to PLC. They didn't quite march through the Inns of Court waving banners, but it was seen as that sort of thing.

Malcolm Harryngton had also been a member of PLC. He was, even then, something of an odd man out. With his pinstripes, waistcoat and fob-chain, in contrast to the off-duty jeans the rest of us wore, and the y in the middle of his name. None of us ever quite understood his interest or his involvement. In the event, we had never been close and had lost contact completely by the end of the decade. We were now to resume acquaintance.

My heavy heinie and I had hung in there till the light was beginning to creep in even to my cave-like abode.

We talked in the darkness. I did not think it would be tactful if, say, Tim Dowell popped into join us. Nor could I afford the risk of his ringing at the bell, and wondering why I refused to open up to him. He was smart enough to work it out for himself.

There were, one could say, three interests at play. Disraeli Chambers' interest in maintaining what was left of their present range of questionable talent. Dowell's in an arrest. Mine in finding out some final answers.

We had, therefore, quite a lot to talk about. He was far more forthcoming than one might have anticipated. Early on, I asked whether he wasn't taking a few more chances on me than I might merit. He didn't answer for a second, then touched with his finger the trigger of his favourite toy.

'You might, well, perhaps, maybe, not have it with you at the time when it mattered. . .'

He smiled. He had such a pleasant smile. It gave me the shits.

'Do you mean in a court?'

'It's not beyond the realms of possibility. . .'

'No, it is not impossible. But I do not think it is likely, do you? That they will keep me alive?'

'I would have thought. . . I don't want to sound naive. . . But. . . Here, in this country, you know. . .'

'It is not here I am wanted. . .'

He was right. Not by Special Branch. Not by the police hierarchy. Only by the drum-busting Sergeant Dowell. Who was now organizing fuzz-rosters to keep the dufuses of Disraeli Chambers alive.

'Still you have not told me what it is you wish to know.'

'I suppose. . . I suppose I'm curious why you agreed to see me, without knowing what I want. . .'

He shrugged. They even did it in Germany. Ich-shrug.

'The game is. . . How shall I say? Drawing to a close, is it not? For a time at least I think we must call it stalemate. . .'

'That didn't stop you last meeting. . .'

181

'Yes. I had my plans. I saw the police, of course. My plan was still working. Why should I stop? Now. I think it is different. They are guarding the bodies, not the office. . .'

He was a realist.

I felt strangely disappointed in him.

I hadn't thought he'd let anything get in his way.

'So you came to see me. . .to break the stalemate?'

'Perhaps. Also. I was curious. You found your way to me. I do not think that was from Keenan. . . Am I correct?'

I nodded. Then asked:

'Mightn't it have been Orbach?'

His face was impassive. I figured. He was trying to decide whether or not to let on that he knew him. It was the first time he acted simply as if I had not spoken. He was to repeat it later.

I started back at square one.

'Why have you been murdering members of Disraeli Chambers?'

'Because they betrayed my comrades. . .'

'What happened?'

He told me about the night they were taken. First he explained some background.

What the press called gangs, revolutionary organizations, fractions or whatever, rarely existed the way they were perceived. A name might be taken: Baader-Meinhof/Red Army Fraction was the best known; a date was a common designation. They did not operate, or subsist, in permanent groups. Rather, individuals, or perhaps a couple, who went their own ways the rest of the time, utilized one such name for a particular action.

It was for this reason that so many managed to evade the law for so long. The police looked for gangs. They knew, of course, the names of individuals and would, as it were, settle for one or two at a time as available. But their operations were oriented towards organizations. When they caught one or two, they could claim no more than limited damage. Only when they caught several at once – enough of whom they could identify with a known group – could they claim destruction.

This was only possible for very short periods. When the people who were to use a gang name for a specific, single purpose first came together, then planned and trained together. It ended when they had struck.

Because the gang would effectively disband immediately after an action, the chances of wholesale conviction were dramatically diminished. One or two might be caught who were linked to this action, or that, or another, or occasionally more than one, but the odds were considerably against the successful capture of a sufficient number to try and tie to a course of conduct over a length of time.

The options for the police were, accordingly, restricted. They could aim to take a small number, who could be convicted of an equally small number of incidents, or they had to hit a larger group at a much earlier stage, before they had together actually committed any offence. This meant there was little chance of conviction, and translated in practice into the alternative of elimination. Once dead, they could be accused, and *in absentia* called to account for, as many charges as the police wanted to claim.

The night it happened was the first night a new grouping – albeit to fly under an existing flag – had gathered.

'How was contact maintained? How did you find each other?'

'There is a network, in Germany, and elsewhere, through which this can happen. These are people who are sympathizers, but not participants. They help us escape, they help us survive, they help us make contact with one another.'

'Lawyers? Are there lawyers amongst these people?'

'I would say, no. Not knowing who we are. Lawyers have their uses, when one is captured. Then, also, they have their job and they understand their position. Before, they are a risk. They do not understand their position. They are frightened. It is harder. . . How shall

I say this? It is hard to play a strange part in a familiar performance, more hard than when you are completely from outside. Do you understand me?'

'I think so.' He meant, I think, that a complete outsider would find everything utterly unreal. He would be compelled to play out the fantasy in itself, without reference to any criteria. It is not a fantasy for a lawyer to have dealings with the wanted. But the way they would be called upon to act, in this contact network, would be different from what they were used to.

They had gone to sleep. There were nine of them. He had heard a noise. He had awoken. He believed it was nerves. He could not get back to sleep. He was lying in the attic. He had gone up on to the roof. Perhaps in order to reassure himself. Perhaps for some fresh air. Perhaps some sixth sense told him to get out. He did not know now which it was. He had saved himself by less than two minutes.

'I did not see anything. I could only hear. They did not shout a warning. They were military. Faces darkened. They came in and the shooting started.'

'Where were you?'

He smiled:

'It is corny. I hid in the chimney.'

'Didn't they look up it?'

'Possibly. It was blocked up at the bottom. At the top there was a cover. I took it off. I climbed in. I pulled the cover back on. It was possible to go across the other roofs. That is what they did. They looked for me. I am sure. They must have seen my sleeping-bag. Empty. But they never looked in the chimney. I was lucky.'

'How long were you there?'

'Nearly two days. I did not dare to come out before. It was cold. I was not properly clothed. I was frightened. Also, I was ashamed. Because I should have warned my comrades, or I should have died with them. Do you not think?'

He was asking me.

I didn't answer. It was way beyond the experiences

I had had, from which I might have guessed what I would have done.

'You haven't told me. . . Why Disraeli Chambers?'

'Ah, yes. Yes. That is your question.'

He paused to collect his thoughts.

'In the evening, when we were eating, Klaus Friske talked of England. He had been in England. In London. He had met some lawyers. Barristers they are called. Keenan. We knew Keenan's name, of course. He had met some colleagues of this Keenan. The woman Creemer. He did not say. But I think he was slept with her.'

Damn me if I wasn't close to correcting his grammar.

'We were amused. They did not know what he was – not a lot. They were like children. They wanted to get close to the fire. But not too close. This is not uncommon. Also in Germany. They can be excited. They think it is dangerous. Glamorous.'

He was bitter:

'They see it for a few minutes or a day. Like the television. They do not live it.'

'Is Helga. . . Like that?'

'No. She is clear. She knows what she will do. She knows what she is believing. Her father. . . Schroeder. . . Perhaps a little bit to make amends. . .'

'Why do you do it?'

I wasn't talking Disraeli Chambers any more.

He thought for a moment, then shrugged again:

'*Ich kann nicht anders. . .*'

To my surprise as much as to his, I remembered. Luther. I can no other.

'You know Luther?'

'I was three years in the seminary. . .'

Holy shit.

I shook my head:

'No, I don't understand. . .'

'Are you a socialist, Mr Woolf?'

'I don't know any more. I used to think so.'

'What do you do?'

'I was a lawyer, too.'

It was all right for me to put it in the past tense. After all, it was my life. I just didn't like it when others did it.

'Now? You are not a lawyer?'

'Nope. I ain't nothing really. I'm doing this job. . . For a relative of someone you killed. . .' I pre-empted his question:

'But in between acts, I tend to do a lot of nothing. . .'

'Yes, I understand. But it is not an easy choice. To do nothing.'

'Is what you do an easy choice?'

'No. But some people – I – cannot do nothing.'

'Was this all you could think of to do?'

I didn't really need to ask. That was what he was saying. His frustration was not different from mine. It was just that he couldn't sit still.

'And now? Why so much time, for such. . . God, they're such petty, pathetic people. . . They can't be worth it!'

He laughed:

'Again. *Ich kann nicht anders.*'

'And, again, I don't understand. . .'

'You see. . . After that night. . . It has not been easy for me. . . To make contacts. . . It has not been possible for me. . . To be involved. Do you see?'

'I think so. You're too badly wanted by the police?'

'No, not at all. This is not a problem. But I am not trusted. . . Now do you see?'

I saw.

'What you said. . . That your friend. . . Klaus? Was that his name. . .'

'Klaus Friske. Yes.'

'Because Klaus had been around Disraeli Chambers just beforehand. . . That's the whole basis for thinking they betrayed you?'

'No. It was a suspicion. Also. I knew. . . We knew. . . There were very few people who could have done this. Who knew where we were, and when. Klaus. . . He did not admit. . . But when he drank. . . In a foreign country one is less careful, yes? With a woman perhaps. . . I think it is likely. . . After, I have had plenty

186

of time to think... I think it must have been from there... Not direct, not deliberate, because they did not know so much, but originally from there or from somewhere close to them... This is what I think for myself...'

'Have you been told it, by anyone else?'

This was another occasion when he acted as if I had not spoken.

'What happened when you saw Keenan? Why did you see him?'

'Helga asked it of me. There was no reason why not.'

'It might have been a set-up?'

'So also you. I take care. With Keenan, also, I take care...'

'Did Helga ask you to see me, or just pass my message on?'

'She passed it on. But I did that for her also. Because you might have come back. Or give her name to the police.'

'Perhaps... But Helga asked you to see Keenan?'

'Yes.'

'And you agreed?'

'Yes. She has been a friend, for many years... A good friend... Perhaps now the only friend...'

'But also a friend of Keenan's?'

'She has many friends...'

Not only Keenan.

'What happened at the meeting?'

'You know, I think, what happened.'

'Did he... He denied it was them?'

'He said so. He said it was not them.'

'But you didn't believe him?'

'No. This is correct. He was... How shall I say? He was hiding something...'

'Did Helga ever ask you to see Russel Orbach?'

I thought for a moment he was going to do his mental disappearing act again. Instead:

'You have asked me before about him. Why?'

'I don't know. It's a feeling. A hunch. He knows a lot.

187

He was one of them. He split up with them. Badly. He hates them. . .'

'It is powerful, hatred. I think, perhaps, the most powerful emotion.'

Before I could stop myself, I said:

'You should know. . .'

'No. This is wrong. I do not hate. I. . . I just do.'

Actions. Not words.

'You didn't answer my question. . .'

'No. She did not ask me.'

'But have you see him? Since?'

I hadn't asked the question. Or. So it seemed from his reaction. I tried a different one.

'Why the last Wednesday? Why always then, their meeting day?'

'This is easy. The first time. This was chance. Coincidence. The man Wishart. After. I can always know, one of them will be there. Yes?'

I had to admit. It is hard to have a meeting with no one present.

'I can be here. Before. I can watch. Choose. Perhaps one, perhaps two, perhaps more. I have the time to understand where they live, how they travel, their movements, their habits. For a little. But enough. Then. On the Wednesday. I have my choice.'

'You. . . I don't believe you could have done it all without some inside information,' I said bluntly.

'Why is this?'

He was a calm bugger all right. About as cold as I felt and as Orbach had acted in Oslo.

'How'd'you know who is who? How'd'you know who was a member at the time? It was Klaus was here, not you. . .'

'Before it was Klaus. After. I have been here after. They are going a lot to meetings, to conferences, to the drinking afterwards. . . Me also.'

'Is it so easy? You can't have used your own name, you must have had to avoid people who knew you. You would have had to come in as a stranger. Is the left that easy to infiltrate?'

188

He laughed bitterly:

'Yes. It is that easy. Consider. It lacks organization, just because it is on the left, it is out of power. It does not have uniform or rank or system. No cards for entry. No security police. When the left gather they might as well do it in the public park. . .

'Also. The left. . . The people are perhaps not so suspicious. In themselves, do you not think, left people are of a nicer. . .' He got lost looking for a word:

'Inclination. Is that the word?'

'Maybe. It'll do. Disposition?'

'Yes, this is the word I am looking for.'

'Your English is pretty damned good.' A lot of it was better than mine.

'I am studying English at university. Then, also, after, in the seminary.'

'OK. . .'

'Perhaps also we can say, because the left always wants more people, they are less careful about who they take. . . Do you think?'

'Maybe. . .'

He was right, though. How many left-wing gatherings had I gone to, where we had behaved as if we were co-conspirators in some secret scheme, and yet I had not known the names of half the people present, let alone what it was that qualified them for admission. Put it the other way round. Who the hell knew who I was half the time, or what I was doing there?

That was how we spent the night. Batting between politics and philosophy, personalities and picking up the details of how he had waged his war. He drank me out of coffee, and I drank me out of all the booze there was left in the flat. I didn't feel even remotely pissed.

'You said. . . You wanted to break the stalemate?'

'Yes. . .'

'Do you think we have?'

'No. Of course not.'

'How did you think it would? Or could?'

'I do not know. Perhaps. Do you think it was from them?' For a second, he was like a little boy, needing to be told he'd done his homework or the washing-up right.

'I don't know. I don't think. . . Well, I don't think you're doing any good. . . I think, maybe, you've made your point. . . You won't get anywhere else with it. . . Who's left to wipe out? Jane Daws? Mike Barron? They're about the only two still around from that time. They ain't worth the effort. They're people of absolutely no consequence. . .'

I felt incredibly alone. Here was I. Sitting with a man who was a murderer. A lot of people would have liked to be in on the interview. I knew now more about what had happened than anyone else – my present companion apart – in the whole world. Yet I felt nothing. I was numbed. Positively anaesthetized. Not just, or perhaps at all, by tiredness. That had come and gone and come and gone it didn't matter any more. But a whole different kind of weariness. I felt, despite myself, utterly indifferent. He could kill Daws, or Barron, and I didn't give a damn. He could get away. It didn't matter. I had discharged my duty to my client.

I couldn't let it go like that. I couldn't just say: later, alligator; thank you and have a nice day; take care on your journey home. The one thing neither he nor I knew was: had his comrades actually been betrayed by Disraeli Chambers, or by someone else? For some reason which I can't explain and I'm not sure I can justify, that alone of all of it still seemed to matter.

He left as suddenly as he had arrived. I was not to tell anyone I had seen him. He promised: he would be in touch again. I had an idea: next time it wouldn't be from across the square. Also, I was by no means sure that our next encounter would be as amicable. Just as I would undoubtedly spend a long time thinking about him, he would be thinking about me. If I had made the slightest slip, or if I now did anything he viewed with suspicion, I knew, from what he had described, how he liked best to express his disapproval.

I slept about three hours. An uneasy sleep riven with images. Everybody was at the party. The living and the dead. No one made any sense. No one seemed to think they needed to, or even ought to try.

Two things he had said stuck in my mind. How it had to be them, or else someone close to them. How easy it is to infiltrate the left.

That was when first a body – in a pin-stripe suit – then a face then finally a name forced their way out of the faculty mockingly known as my memory. Malcolm Harryngton.

I'd caught the story long after I'd left PLC. It had first been run in one of the London weekly listings magazines, which incorporated a few pages of hard news. It had been taken up by the Guardian newspaper, in the context of a larger piece on infiltration. It must have been back in 1979 or 1980, and my only interest was because I recognized Harryngton's name.

He was alleged to have been an establishment informer against left-wing legal activism. PLC wasn't mentioned. It could not itself have been the subject of his attention. Rather, a way of meeting those on its left who, in turn, might wearing other hats be involved in the sort of adventure his masters wanted to know about. For example, members of Disraeli Chambers. I even had a vague idea Keenan had figured in one or other of the articles, offering – as usual – his opinion.

I couldn't get to the *Guardian* in time to use their library that day. I rang Sandy. She didn't remember him at all well, could add nothing to what I had already recalled for myself. Anne Godwin and Gerry Gilligan had never known him. I wasn't ready to try the name out on the two people at the centre who would certainly have been around at the same time, and whose memories, in sharp contrast to my own, were elephantine. Keenan. And Orbach.

After my weekly fix on Hill Street Blues, I mooched round to Lewis's. I wasn't looking for Tim Dowell, especially, though I wouldn't have minded if he'd been there to keep me company. I was beginning to miss him. It felt like it had been a long time.

What I wanted was a word with the man himself.

'All alone tonight, then, Dave?' Lewis leered.

'Looks that way. . .'

'I'll buy you a drink if you don't tell Dowell. . .'

We were served by a male waiter. Young. Slicked back black hair. Tight trousers. After he left us, Lewis said:

'Teaching him the business, you might say. . .' I was intended to spot the double meaning.

'First time you came in here looking for me. . . You said I might want a favour from you some day. Do you remember?'

I grunted non-committally. Not until I knew what the favour was.

'What is Tim Dowell up to?'

'Why do you ask?'

'He's been coming here a great deal. Not just with you,' he added archly, as if it might make me jealous:

'In the past, whenever he came, he had a purpose in mind. He wanted something. Now, he sits and drinks, and watches. Me. The waitresses. The other customers.'

It was quite an admission. He was spooked.

'Maybe he fancies you, Lewis,' I was feeling bold.

He looked pained:

'I am trusting you, Dave. Do you understand what that means? Do you understand how rarely I do that? Do you understand?'

I was not to joke.

'Sorry.'

I actually did feel it. He was showing his age. There were at least ten wrinkles now where there'd only been nine and three-quarters before.

'Maybe he's just unhappy. He's. . . Well. . .'

I didn't want to be disloyal to Dowell either.

'He ain't exactly got the confidence of his superiors any more. . .'

'It's this business with the barristers, isn't it? Are you involved in it, Dave? How much do you know?'

'Not a whole bunch. You helped us out. You knew before anyone else anyway. . .' When he'd told us Art Farquharson wasn't a fag-killing.

He shivered at the memory.

Not with fear. But. Excitement.

'I don't like it, Dave. It isn't natural. Murdering lawyers. I mean. They could get scared. Then where would we be? Who'd we go to?'

I laughed:

'I don't think this lot would've been your scene anyway, Lewis. . . Strictly political.'

He tutted. He didn't approve of politics. They weren't natural, either.

'Is that it? Is it political?'

It wasn't so much that I wanted to pay off the old favour, as that I had another in mind:

'Yes. Heavily.'

He breathed out. At least it was nothing that would interfere with business.

He enjoyed being informed.

'Lewis. . .'

Despite myself, I dropped my voice. It was not so much caution, as nerves.

'Would you. . . How would I. . . Lewis. . . I'm not a little scared myself. . . I want. . . I need. . . Oh, shit. . .'

He tutted again. I guess he thought bad language wasn't natural too.

'I want a gun. . .'

There. I'd said it.

The ceiling didn't fall.

The only thing I was frightened of was: that he'd say yes.

'You want a gun? You, Dave? Want a gun?'

He was like a stuck record.

I knew what he was thinking. I was a sometime lawyer, turned highly qualified process-server, whose most dangerous activity hitherto had been the quantities I could consume of Southern Comfort.

'That's what I said. . . I want a gun.' I felt stronger about it now I knew a bolt of lightning wouldn't strike me dead for saying it.

He thought some more about it.

'Do you know how to use a gun, Dave?'

'Sure. I watch Hill Street Blues every week. You sort of, well, crouch down behind something, or someone, and point it, don't you?'

'It isn't a laughing matter, my friend. . .'

I declare. He was genuinely concerned about me.

'No, I know. But. . . There's people around. . . There's been a lot of killing.'

'Has anyone been threatening you, Dave? Why don't you let me take care of them for you. . .'

I couldn't dream what I'd owe him if I did.

'They're not your scene, Lewis. Like I said. Political.'

He knew what I meant. He'd seen The Long Good Friday. The one where the gangsters get into a war with the IRA. The gangsters lose.

'They're crazy. . .'

Politicals. Terrorists. He didn't say what he meant but we were both talking about the same thing.

'Got no respect. . . Just crazy.'

'Now'd'you see why?'

'You ought to keep out of it, Dave. It's not your scene either. . .' What he meant was. I couldn't handle it.

'I. . . Uh. . . I don't think, you know, in a shoot out or something like that, sure. . . But, well, I'd just feel better, you know? A sort of comforter. . .'

'Try sucking your thumb. . . Or. . .' He grinned.

Which told me.

I could have what I wanted.

'And ammunition?'

'I'll tell you what I'll do. I'll load it for you. Just the once. I'll show you how it works. Just the once. But that's it. . .'

'How much is it going to cost me?'

He held up the fingers and thumb of one hand. I blanched. It was five day's work. Still. I might be able to claim it on expenses. Or use it in trade when I'd finished the job and started to spend the loot I'd earned. If, that is, I was around to do so.

I didn't see Harryngton until after the next weekend. On the Monday. Which put us two days away from the next chambers' meeting. I saw him at four-thirty. Traditionally the barristers' conference time. When they've finished for the day in court.

He hadn't changed much. A bit plumper. More prosperous. I didn't like to ask but wasn't the gold chain silver the last time I saw him.

'I haven't seen you for a long time. . . Are you still practising?'

I didn't bore him with my usual rejoinder.

'You're obviously doing well. Still enjoying it?'

'The old cut and thrust, eh. . .'

He'd make a good coroner. They had the same sort of style.

'Are you still a member of PLC?'

He frowned:

'No. I left.'

'Why?'

'I think you know,' he pursed his lips:

'What do you want to see me about?' He'd frozen over.

I thought of saying: I think you know.

'That, I guess. You've. . . Uh. . . Read about Disraeli Chambers?'

'Of course.' Who hadn't, in and around the profession. If they could've got cover like this for being alive, they'd've all earned enough to retire by now.

'I've been interested in it.'

'Interested?' He knew I didn't meant I was an avid reader of the newspapers.

'Investigating. . .around it. For a client. A relative of one of the members. Late members.'

He inclined his head graciously, as if to say: I am prepared to respect your reasons for asking questions.

'How can I help you, then? I am, as you know, not on friendly terms with them. . .'

'You were around, with some of them a few years ago. Keenan. Orbach.'

He shook his head:

'I didn't know Orbach. I might have seen him once or twice. He was not as active as Keenan. Keenan was

195

at PLC a lot. And. . .at other meetings. But Orbach's no longer there, didn't you know that?'

'Yes, I knew. So you haven't seen him, recently?'

'At court once or twice, possibly. Not to speak to. I suppose, we nod when we pass. . .'

'And Keenan? Do you nod at him?'

He chuckled:

'I would say, no, we are not even on nodding terms. . .'

'Why not?'

'Again, you know that. You know what was said about me.'

'You didn't sue. . .'

'What for? Being accused of being in some sort of relationship with the authorities is hardly libellous. Libel has to lower you in the eyes of right-thinking members of society, you know. . . I was only lowered in the eyes of the left,' he smiled thinly at the jocular way he had put what was not a joke.

What I wanted to know was: how much truth was there in what they had written? It was likely to be the last question I'd be able to put. I wasn't banking on an answer. I slipped another in first.

'How close were you to Keenan?'

'For a short time, we were friendly. He came to my house for dinner, with his wife. Some people. . . People like yourself I would say. . . Found me an unusual type to have an interest in PLC and the movement. . . I could say: that was your prejudice. He didn't have that sort of prejudice. After all, we weren't so dissimilar although he was and is of course much better known and much more successful than I. . . Professionally as well as politically. . .'

'Did you go there?'

'Where? To his house? Yes. There were a few meetings. . . I dropped in on a couple of occasions. . .' He chuckled again:

'Lady Helen. . . As they say, quite a lady. . .'

He was no gentleman.

Except.

When I asked that final question.
He told me no lies.
Just like a gentleman.
Instead.
He invited me to leave his room.
To put it another way.
He told me to get the hell out.

Chapter Twelve

He caught up with me as I left Kentish Town station, on my way to Sandy's.

'You will see your friend. . .' He sounded jealous. Wistful. It ain't no fun giving up all aspects of a normal life. Staking everything on one type of action, with the probability of just one way for it all to end. Knowing that must happen. Waiting for it. For that time when he'd be able to do what he couldn't do now. Nothing.

'I will see my friend. . .'

'Have you told her you have seen me?'

'No.'

I wasn't lying.

Automatically, we had cut down an alley.

He checked behind us.

'I'm not being followed. . .'

'I have followed you. . .'

'Since when?'

'Since yesterday morning. . .'

I shivered.

'Who was this you are seeing?'

'A barrister. Not a member of Disraeli Chambers.'

'And which is his name?'

He produced from his pocket a sheet of paper on to which – presumably while he had waited for me to come out again – he had copied the names from the boards which all barristers maintain outside their chambers.

I picked one at random.

Not Malcolm Harryngton.

A woman's name.

I hoped she didn't have two young children and a dog.

Quickly, I added:

'She is nothing to do with this. An old friend,' I laughed nervously:

'Because of Sandy. . . I had to see her. Do you understand?'

He didn't believe me. I didn't blame him. It wasn't a good story.

He said:

'It is tomorrow. . .'

Wednesday. The last in the month.

'And?'

We understood one another. He wanted an end to the stalemate. I wanted an end to this job. We both got what we wanted when we finally knew for sure who had betrayed his comrades. I said:

'I have to see Keenan. . . He's the only one who can help. . .'

Then he surprised me:

'Are you sure?'

The name he'd ignored the other night.

I glanced down at his holdall.

He followed my eyes.

So long as he was carrying it, I could not give him the chance.

'Where?' He asked.

I looked long and pointedly at the bag again.

'No bag.'

'Do you promise?'

It was kind of pathetic. I had no other way. Though he might be a killer, he had shown no evidence of being in any way dishonest.

'I promise.'

'Both of them. . . That's what you want, isn't it?'

He nodded slowly.

I felt an almost sexual excitement. It was what I wanted too. It had become what I needed.

I could hardly get the word out:

'Sandy's. . .'

199

'Tonight. It must be tonight. After nine o clock. Perhaps much later. You understand me. Perhaps you must wait all the night.'

'I understand. . .'

'Do you promise, also?'

He meant: no set-up.

'I promise.'

'Go. . .'

I went.

Sandy wasn't home, I let myself in.

I had a lot to do.

I had to get Keenan there.

And Orbach.

And keep Sandy out.

She was still at the office. I caught her on the private number.

'I want you to do something for me. . . Two things, really. . .'

'What?'

'Will you ring Keenan? Find him. . . Wherever. . . Get him to come here. . . Before nine o clock. . . Can you do that?'

I didn't like the reasons why I knew she could.

'You said two things. . .'

'I'd like it. . .if you didn't come back tonight.'

She whistled through her teeth. It scratched in my ear.

'You'n'Alex, huhn? Who'd've thunk it?' She was playing for time.

'Well, you know, I guess I need a little variety. . .'

I could say that to her. She knew proof positive I didn't.

'Dave. . . Are you in. . . Well, are you in danger?'

Who? Me? Ha! What a joke! Danger? What was danger to a man of my calibre and experience? What did I care if a gang of German gunmen burst into her house and ventilated it with sub-machine guns? I could handle that shit. Wasn't I Captain Furillo and Clint Eastwood and Mick Belcher rolled into one? Ain't she never heard of Krypton?

200

'I think. . . No, there's no danger,' I lied:

'I wouldn't ask, otherwise, you know, for you to get Keenan here. . .'

I figure she was weighing up: just how much of a bastard was I capable of?

'Why can't I be there, Dave?'

So, already, she wasn't stupid.

'I just think. . . You know. . . The things that are going to be said. . . It'll be pretty heavy. . .'

She was silent for a moment.

Then:

'If I can find him, I'll get him there. . .'

On the other, she had no comment.

I waited for her to ring back and confirm she'd clicked with Keenan. Immediately after, I rang Orbach.

I'd been much more concerned about finding Keenan. He had a thousand and fifty things to do every day. Meetings. Speeches. Wife and children. Chambers. Somewhere in between, I knew it was also his habit to wangle a woman if he could. Orbach was very different. He left work as early as he was able. Sped home. Shut the world out behind him. And sat, looking at the empty space behind the trees.

'I want to see you,' I sounded as terse as I felt.

After a pause, he said:

'I'm at home. . .'

'I want to see you here. . .'

'Where's here?'

I told him. Adding:

'It's not far. . .'

'Yes, I know that. Why do you want me there?'

'I don't know what time, but I'm going to get a call, here, tonight. A foreign call. To be precise, from Germany.' I meant it to sound like 'phone call. Otherwise, it was near enough to true. These other guys. They'd all been running around, making an arsehole out of me, telling me half-truths, or omitting essential information, but always reserving to themselves the gentleman's privilege of saying that they had not lied.

He hesitated longer than the time before. But he couldn't resist.

Sandy had told Keenan to be there at eight thirty. I asked Orbach to arrive at nine. It was cutting it fine, but I didn't doubt we were in for a long wait. He would probably be watching the premises even now, perhaps he had followed me straight back, so as to ensure I didn't pack the house with police before his arrival. He would want to be as sure as the circumstances permitted prior to his entry.

I didn't actually care who came first. I only didn't want them bumping into each other on the doorstep. If either of them saw the other before coming in, there was a real risk he'd walk away. Once I had them inside, I was going to keep them together. If necessary, with a little help from my (new) friend.

I had an hour to kill. Pardon. To waste. You think I'm going to tell you I took a belt or two to bolster my courage. You'd be wrong. More like a full tumbler.

By quarter to nine, Keenan was still no-show. I was beginning to sweat. When the doorbell rang, I ran to open up, grab whoever was out there – I swear I didn't care which – and pull him inside.

It was Keenan. He was, of course, more than a little surprised, and not a little disconcerted, to see me:

'Sandy. . .'

'Yes, I know. I asked her to.'

It wasn't, I suppose, tactful. I couldn't help reminding him.

He didn't like being conned. Maybe he would've walked. I told him it was no more than slight redress:

'I liked Oslo. . .'

He shrugged. That was over.

'Would you like a drink?'

'You still haven't said what you want. . .'

'No more I have. I wanted to talk with you. Away from your chambers. Away from your home.' It was the second place I mentioned that caused his face muscles to tighten up.

'OK. . . Scotch and water. . .'

I was in the kitchen fetching the water when the doorbell rang again. I cut straight out into the hall, which left him in the living-room, to let in the next contestant.

'This way, please,' I said, before he had a chance to speak, and Keenan to hear his voice.

The way they stared at each other wasn't the way Livingstone must've stared at Stanley. More like the way Hitler might've felt if Churchill had walked into the Berlin bunker shortly after he'd swallowed his cyanide brew.

It was Orbach spoke first:

'Alex. It's been a long time.'

I held my breath.

And, inside my jacket, my gun.

You could see Keenan mentally tossing a coin. Deep inside he had wanted this confrontation for a long time.

'Russel. . .'

They were stalking around each other like prize cocks.

Then Keenan grinned, and held out a hand.

Orbach accepted.

'Now what?' He asked me.

'Now we talk. . . But. . . A drink?'

I still hadn't brought Keenan his.

Orbach shook his head.

He wanted it clear.

Keenan was still wearing a suit. He had, presumably, been in court earlier that day. Had no chance to change. Orbach, on the other hand, had been at home when I caught him. He was wearing a Norwegian knitted cardigan, with silver-plated buckles down the front.

'I've had an interesting couple of discussions recently, with a pair of Germans,' I opened once we were all settled down.

Neither batted an eyelid.

I had to remember. I was dealing with two, highly experienced barristers. Not just barristers, but Queen's Counsel, the alleged cream of the cream. They were, probably, amongst the cleverest people I had ever known. Perhaps the cleverest of all. It was more likely true of Orbach than Keenan. But with Orbach present, Keenan was on his mettle too. I was not going to score heavily by trick questions or shock tactics.

I still wasn't near expecting my visitor. To my surprise, though less to theirs who knew it wasn't my place, I heard a key slide into the lock. I was so stunned it took me a minute to get up and go for the door. Sandy came straight in. She looked at me defiantly. Her home.

'Alex,' she acknowledged:

'Russel. We haven't met for a long time. . .'

'True,' he said:

'I seem to recall you stopped briefing me several years ago. . .'

Sandy flushed.

My face asked what was this about. Orbach explained, matter-of-factly:

'After the split, a lot of people lined up behind Disraeli Chambers. They'd heard the rumours. Decided I must be in the wrong. None of them came to ask me of course. Suddenly, I was no longer the lawyer I'd been the day before.'

'Russel. . . It's long ago. . . You've done well. . .' Alex said.

I'd forgotten. Keenan had once been Orbach's pupil-master. He had a history of authority to dip into when it suited.

Orbach wasn't impressed:

'Everything I did, I worked for, Alex. Nothing was handed me on a platter. . .'

Sandy had gone out to the kitchen. She could still hear. She came back in, shaking her head:

'Russel, Russel. You don't need to be jealous of him any more. . .'

She was right. On both counts. He was jealous. And. He didn't need to be.

Alex tried once more to take command:

'Dave, you asked us both here. What for? For this? You said. . . You had seen some Germans. . .'

I wasn't sorry to see the set swivel in my direction. Like Sandy, I did not find the sight of two middle-aged men bickering like school-children exactly edifying.

'Yes. Helga Schroeder was one of them. . .'

Orbach and Keenan exchanged a glance.

'Who was the other?' Keenan asked.

'I don't know his name. . .' I grinned:

'But we all know who I mean. . .'

'I'm glad if they do, but. . .' Sandy said pointedly.

'Sandy. I said you shouldn't be here. . .'

'I'm here. It's my home. You're my lover. You're my friend,' she told Keenan, consolingly rather than rubbing salt in that particular wound:

'I'm entitled. . .'

Orbach explained:

'He's seen the man who committed the murders. That's right, isn't it, Dave?'

'Yes.'

'You said you were expecting a 'phone call tonight, from Germany, was that true or was that just to get me here?'

'It wasn't what I said. I said a call. Not a 'phone call. . .'

'Ah. . . I see. . .'

Orbach was the only one to do so. He relaxed. He, at least, planned to enjoy himself.

It was exactly then that he arrived. He banged hard on the door, instead of ringing the bell. I shot up to let him in. He brushed past me, immediately flinging open other doors. Not just doors to rooms – the kitchen, the bathroom, the bedrooms, – but also to cupboards within.

As promised, he was not carrying his holdall.

It took him several minutes to complete his search, satisfy himself the house was clean.

Then, he smiled at Keenan, and held out a hand which, with obvious reluctance, Alex shook:

'We meet again,' the German said.

Alex didn't answer.

'Hello, Hans.' Russel, too, held out a hand, which

the man whose first name I now had for the first time, took.

Hans bowed slightly, politely, to Sandy:

'We have not met. But, I think, we have spoken. . .'

She was the most ill-at-ease. The least involved. Accordingly, the one with the greatest amount of spare attention, to concentrate on the less salubrious aspect of the encounter. To wit. That the man she was now entertaining in her home was a murderer.

'Can I. . . Would anyone like a drink, or a coffee? Something to eat. . .' Heredity told. At a time like this, she could resort only to the as yet unfulfilled role of Jewish momma.

'Sit,' Hans ordered.

Heredity told again. She sat.

'Now?' He looked at me.

It was my show.

I'd just begun to wonder whether it was that good a play after all. Which was, now I'd finally got the curtain unstuck, a little late in the day.

'I would say. . . You want to know who betrayed your comrades. . .'

'I know who. . .'

'I don't think so. . . You thought you knew who. . . You had some reason for what you thought. . . That was the way you put it, wasn't it Russel?'

Orbach smiled pleasantly.

He didn't care what happened. He just didn't care. He'd got his confrontation with Keenan. All the bitterness and the pain accumulated over those years since he was ousted from the group would find some sort of resolution tonight.

'I think. . . I'd say it was not a bad guess. . . But it wasn't quite right. You were encouraged to think it. . . By Orbach. . . Correct?'

Hans didn't answer, so Orbach did it for him:

'He presented me with a theory, of how it had happened. It would be correct to say. . . I never disabused him of it. . .'

'Why not?' I snapped.

'I think. . . I think that is not for me to say. I was, of course, and am under no duty – legally – to tell Hans anything. . .' He was pointing out, accurately so far as I could tell, that he had committed no crime by failing to correct the German.

'Would you not say. . . A duty to tell the police what you knew? Of meeting Hans. . .'

'This is the first time we have met in this country, Dave. . .'

'Ah, Oslo,' I hadn't thought of that.

I remembered what Helen Keenan had said about Orbach. The great manipulator. Whether or not it had been true prior to his fall from grace at Disraeli Chambers, he had made it true since. This was his revenge. Gilligan said he was viewed as a devil. Already condemned as such, he had nothing left to lose by acting like one. He was probably telling the truth when he claimed not to have told Hans it was them; but it was just as true it was his responsibility that Hans went on thinking it.

'What you do not tell me, Mr Woolf, is if I am right. . . if Russel is right,' he looked straight at Orbach, without anger, but also without his customary smile. He was confirming Orbach's role in leading him on.

'If I can adopt what Russel just said, I don't think that's for me to say. . .'

Which left Keenan.

He was white as a sheet.

'Shall I help you, Alex?' I asked gently.

He shook his head:

'Don't. Please.'

From his coat pocket, Hans produced a pistol. I cursed:

'You promised. . .'

'Come, Mr Woolf. I promised only the other gun. This. . .' He held it up for all to see. I was already aware it was in a different class from that with which Lewis had provided me. The difference was between a three-legged race and the Olympic marathon.

He placed it gingerly on his lap.

'Now. . . Alex. . . Please,' he prompted.

'Cat got your tongue, Alex,' Orbach hissed:

'Or a bitch?'

'You bastard. . .' Keenan spat back at his oldest friend:

'You would have told him, wouldn't you. . . In the end, after the others had been. . .finished. . . Wouldn't you?' He shouted, half-rising in his chair until Hans motioned with the weapon for him to resume his seat.

Orbach shook his head slowly:

'I don't know, Alex. I really don't know. I didn't tell him. Did I? I could have told him, anyway. . .'

'Oh, no, you couldn't. He wouldn't't've bothered, with the others. . .' He was shaking:

'Wishart. Carrie. Jackdaw. Art. Harry. You killed them, you did. . .' He was almost weeping.

'No, Alex,' Orbach remained calm:

'You. You far more than me. We both knew. All along. But it was your responsibility to tell him. Not mine. All you did was remain silent. Like you always did. Like you did. . .over me.'

'How could I?' Keenan was openly crying now:

'How could I?' I. I. I. It echoed round the room.

Hans spoke softly:

'Now you will tell me. . .'

He was asking me.

I told him the story of the left-wing infiltrator called Harryngton with a y. Who'd gotten close to Keenan. Closer still to the Lady H. Close enough that one night chatting as even the most ill-suited and casual of lovers will do, she told him what she'd heard from Keenan, who'd himself heard it from Creemer, about a clandestine left-wing gathering in Germany.

She had not noticed at the time when he pressed for further details. What city? Really, how courageous, he must have replied. What sort of house, what sort of locality. She didn't know what it was like. I know the town. Do you know an address? She mentions the area. Perhaps he says: that's clever; middle-class area; the police'll never find them.

She'd known afterwards, of course. When the two stories about Harryngton hit the papers and Keenan had brought them back, to share chagrin at having been taken in. That was when she would have told him. How badly they'd been taken in, how far she'd let him in. What they'd talked about that last night they'd slept together.

And Keenan, in turn, had told the only friend in whom he confided just about everything. The only member – as he then still was – of his chambers who might just possibly be as strong as Keenan himself, on occasion perhaps stronger. Even father-figures need a daddy to turn to once in a while.

'I told you she was poison, Alex. . . I said she'd bring us both down in the end. . .'

Keenan covered his face with his hands. He'd been trapped. Orbach was right. It was his responsibility to let the Germans know how it had happened, once his comrades had started catching deadly consequences. He had had the means. Through Helga Schroeder. But he had spent his whole life protecting Lady Helen against her own follies. It was a habit he didn't know how to stop.

The smile had gone – I had the premonition for the last time – from Hans' face. He lifted the gun. Not as if he was about to use it. To remind us all. Not even that he had it. But that this was his way.

'You. . . All of you. . .'

I didn't have the courage to invite him to exclude Sandy. Or me.

I scratched my stomach, inside my jacket, until the back of my nail struck against the butt of Lewis' gun.

'You have played with me. . .'

Keenan shook his head:

'It wasn't. . . That wasn't my intention. . .'

Orbach smiled thinly. He wasn't about to deny it. He'd played with all of them. He still didn't give a damn what happened.

I glanced at Sandy. She was biting her lower lip. Scared. I mouthed:

'I'm sorry. . .'

She smiled back, though a little sadly, as if to say: I don't blame you.

'What happens now?' Orbach asked cheerfully.

I glanced at my watch. It was half past eleven. I said: 'Nothing. . . For half an hour. . .'

No one got it, except Hans.

It still didn't reinstate his smile.

He explained:

'Wednesday. It is Wednesday in half an hour. Yes. I think Mr Woolf is right. . .'

We had some sort of reprieve.

Not a long one.

It felt like a year we sat in silence. It was no more than ten minutes. Everybody was thinking. None of us believed Hans would simply walk away from it. He had gone too far to leave the job unfinished. Logic gave him Keenan. He was the only one still in the chambers, and of everyone present the man with the greatest responsibility for the betrayal with which it had all started.

But it was Orbach who had led him astray. Let him waste his efforts on a bunch of people who had been as innocuously inactive in this matter as in any other. In so doing, he had diverted him from his true target.

Orbach said, to Keenan, as if Hans was not there:

'No, Alex, I would never have told him. I couldn't have done that. . .'

Keenan nodded. He knew it was true.

'Do you remember. . . When everything was happening at chambers. . . There was a letter, I'd written you and Helen. . . A personal letter. . . You handed round for them to read?'

'Yes. I'm sorry. That was wrong.'

'It doesn't matter now. The point is. Afterwards when everyone around us was working up a lather about how terrible I was and what I'd done, you wrote me a letter. Also a personal letter. What you wrote meant you never believed what Helen said. You signed it with love. I never used that, on you. . .'

210

A letter like that would have upset everybody's apple cart. Maybe, after all, Tim Dowell had a point. That Orbach had wanted it to happen. Had perhaps engineered it.

Keenan nodded again. They had fought their war, like opposing generals who had studied together at the same military academy, and who had for each other not merely respect but affection. They had done anything they could to destroy the enemy army, but always seeking to protect from harm those feelings of friendship for each other.

'I do not want to hear of this,' Hans hissed:

'This is not for your quarrel. . . It is for mine. . .'

'I don't know, Hans,' Orbach spoke as if they were discussing which film to go to, rather than arguing for their – our! – lives:

'It's all about betrayal. . .'

'How can you. . . What they did to you. . . How can you consider that with what they did to us?'

Orbach shrugged:

'Sure, it wasn't at the same level. But the point's the same, isn't it? Betrayal by those you have every reason to trust. Betrayal by those who have claimed and received your respect and your confidence because of what they say they stand for. Betrayal by your own side is so much more embittering than betrayal by your known enemies. Betrayal by hypocrites sheltering behind false masks. . . What does it matter for which betrayal they were destroyed? The point is. . .that they had to be destroyed. . . Isn't it?'

He asked the last question not of the German but of Keenan.

'God, no, Russel. . . God, no, they didn't have to be destroyed. . . They never did anyone any harm. . .'

'Or good. . .'

'So what? So what if that's true. . . That they never did anyone any good. . . Did they deserve to die for that?'

'That's not what I'm saying. For claiming to do good . . For the lie of the claim. . . For that. . .'

211

'You, Hans, you do not agree with him! You cannot agree with him! What you have done, with your life, what your comrades did, before they died... It had nothing to do with this! That is the betrayal... You, too, have been betrayed...' He started to laugh, close to hysteria:

'Now we're all equal. We've all been betrayed. By each other.'

'Oh, God, please,' Sandy spoke:

'Please... Please Hans... I'm going to be... I have to...'

She was clutching her side, like she was having a seizure.

I went to her, put my arm around her.

'I have to go...'

'Let her go, to the toilet, Hans, please...' I begged.

He hesitated.

Then. Nodded yes.

She ran off into the kitchen.

I got there a split second before he did.

After all. I had been half-living in the house for several weeks, while he'd only been around the once, and layout wasn't what concerned him. The way to the toilet was through the hall. The kitchen led only to the back door.

He rose from his seat waving the gun.

There was Keenan.

And Orbach.

And.

Me.

Had I betrayed him too?

He was spoiled rotten for choice.

It was like a tableau.

We were all frozen in position.

I was still crouched by the chair Sandy had been occupying.

Keenan had half-risen at the same time as Hans.

Orbach sat unmoved, and unmoving, exactly as he had throughout.

I grabbed for my gun.

A familiar voice screamed:

'Armed police. . .'

Then.

Everything was happening at once.

I never heard so much noise.

Suddenly.

It was just like someone switched the television off.

My last thought before I lost consciousness was.
Damn. Now I'll have to wait till next week to see what
happens.

It was only until the next day.

I woke in hospital.

I was in a private room.

I couldn't feel my right arm.

I wasn't too sure how much of the rest of me was still
there either.

After a couple of minutes, I started to hurt.

I figured out what had happened.

I'd got shot.

I was relieved at least my keen intellect was still alive.

The door opened.

Sandy came in, carrying flowers.

'Shit. . . I must be dying. . .'

She laughed:

'I thought it'd be nice to have something pretty to
look at while I waited. . .'

'Other than me, huh?'

She put the flowers down, sat on the side of the bed
and, cautiously, kissed me gently on the lips:

'I'm sorry,' she said.

She was sorry?

'It was my fault, really,' came a voice from the door:

'My persuasive skills, you know. . .'

'How you doing, Tim?'

'Fine. . . You?'

'I don't know. You tell me.'

'Nothing serious. Grazed a bone. Maybe took a bit out
of it. You won't notice.'

'Great. . . Make sure they keep it. . . I'll send it to

Mrs Nicholas.'

'I spoke to her,' Sandy said:

'She was very upset. I got the impression she sort of liked you. . .'

'Yeah. Some people do. I'm an acquired taste.'

After a bit, I asked:

'Someone going to tell me what happened?'

Sandy explained:

'He came to see me. He said you were in a lot of trouble. He told me you'd gone and got a gun. I was frightened, Dave. When you rang me, at the office, asking to get Alex there, I called him. . .'

'Not bad for a roster organizer?' I addressed the graduate officer.

'Well, maybe I wasn't exactly completely confined to that job. . .'

'I knew you were lying, when Lewis said how much you'd been hanging around. Why?'

'Give the kraut a chance to get next to you. . .'

'And all that guff about Gimbo?'

'No, that was true. He's pissing himself. . .'

'And?'

'I was in Sandy's garden. . . Came through a house in the street behind. . . With, er, well, a couple of colleagues. . . We had more in the streets around. . . As soon as Sandy opened the door, we moved. . . They were coming in the front at the same time. . .'

'You still haven't told me yet. . .'

Who got who.

Dowell breathed on his knuckles and rubbed his lapels. He'd got Hans.

'Poor bastard. . . Still, I suppose it was what he wanted . . . The others?'

'Nope. You were the only other one got hurt. . .'

They would have to live with it. It would get out. One way or another. These things always did.

'He made a terrible mess of the house,' Sandy commented:

'Before they got him. . .'

'I thought. . . I shot. . .'

214

'Yeah. We pulled your bullet out of the ceiling plaster. . .'

Oh. Uh. Not exactly marksmanlike.

Sandy asked:

'I was right, Dave, wasn't I? You couldn't've handled it. . .'

I looked at her, my mouth agape:

'Me? Not handle it? Huh! No sweat. If you'd left well alone, I wouldn't be in this mess now. . .'

'You'd be in a fucking coffin,' Dowell said.

'Exactly. What's this room cost? Who's going to pay for it?'

'I'll advance it, out of your salary,' Sandy smiled:

'How about it, Dave? You're no detective.'

I scowled:

'The hell I'm not. . . Where's my next case?'

Dowell laughed:

'I'd wait a bit, if I were you. Think about it. I mean. Just for the first time. Ever. Think about it before you do it.'

He got up and, glancing covertly at the door, slipped something out from beneath his jacket:

'I don't know what this'll do to you. . .'

He'd brought in a half of the only true comfort I ever knew.

'But since you didn't get killed in her house, I thought you'd like another chance here. . .'

Sandy snatched it from him.

I held out my only working hand, pleading.

'Uhuh,' she shook her head:

'Me first. I'm finally going to find out what this stuff tastes like. . .'

I suppose. She was right. She might as well.

CONTROLLING INTEREST

Bernard Bannerman

'The body of a woman solicitor was discovered by staff arriving yesterday morning at the Holborn offices of the prestigious London solicitors, Mather's. Katrina Pankhurst, 32, had been shot. Police are investigating.'

A murder on the premises is bad news for a law firm. It discourages clients. It also discourages recruits which is damaging to a firm like Mather's with a reputation, a lot of clients, but very few partners. But, as Dave Woolf, one-time lawyer, part-time boozer and (almost) full-time private eye realizes, a thorough professional would prefer a murder to a leak any day of the week.

Also by Bernard Bannerman in Sphere Books:

THE LAST WEDNESDAY

CRIME
0 7474 0383 X